"*The Dream Dimensions* is an absolute must-read for anyone enchanted by the wild, wondrous realm of dreams and magick. This is a truly well-written story that's as gripping as it is profound. As someone who lives for exploring dreamscapes, I'm blown away by how Megan so artfully spins the mystical into something so vivid and down-to-earth—it feels like she's speaking straight to your soul. A true page turner, I couldn't put it down! This book is a sparkling gem, igniting curiosity about the unseen and leaving you hungry for more." - Pippa Oona PhD, Metaphysical Minister and Author of *A Map of Secret Rivers, How to Navigate Timelines*

"*The Dream Dimensions* is a spellbinding journey where mystery, magick, and metaphysics entwine. Through Hannah's quest, we are reminded that ancestral wisdom lives in our bones and dreams, waiting to be awakened. This story not only entertains but also whispers truths about healing, ancestry, and the hidden forces shaping our lives. I personally love the galactic connection." - Dr. Lisa Thompson, Bestselling Author of *Connection to the Cosmos, Wisdom of the Galactics, and Awakening to Your Multidimensional Self*

"A luminous conclusion to the trilogy, weaving prophecy, alchemy, and ancestral remembrance into a tale that transcends time and space. Both haunting and empowering, this story awakens the reader to their own inner light—lingering long after the last page is turned." - Jamie Vos Love, Galactic Channeler and Author of *Love is The Code*

THE DREAM DIMENSIONS

A Metaphysical Mystery of Magick

Megan Mary

INNER REALMS PUBLISHING

For more information contact: Inner Realms Publishing info@innerrealmspublishing.com

MeganMary.com

Book cover by Dragana Nikolic

Illustration by Melissa Rankin

Editing by Ivywild Editing & Writing Services LLC and Edit Experts

979-8-9990811-2-4 (hardcover)

979-8-9990811-3-1 (dustjacket)

979-8-9990811-1-7 (paperback)

979-8-9990811-0-0 (ebook)

Library of Congress Control Number: 2025917557

To my husband, for graciously allowing me the space and time to publish this trilogy within 365 days, in my own race-against-time. We've come a very long way and the best is yet to come.

CONTENTS

CHAPTER ONE

THE RITUAL

OCTOBER 24, 2013

A thick fog crept across the dewy ground as the waning moon rose high in the sky. Cresting over the tops of the maple trees, branches dark as ink reached up and out across the sky. In the furthest, highest reaches of Skye Manor, inside the secret turret room, Hannah Skye and Ashlin Aldona stood in darkness, surrounded by candles.

Within the sacred circle, Hannah began, "I now proclaim this space protected. Only the highest and brightest may be present. No darkness shall dwell here nor attach itself," Hannah declared.

"I call in the spirits of the four directions: North, South, East, and West. I call in the four elements of this earthly plane: Earth, Air, Fire, and Water. I call upon my spirit guides, large and small, to stand with us. And I call upon my ancestors, the legacy of Skye, and those beyond to support us." She waved her hands in the air, spun around, and then bowed.

Ashlin was sitting cross-legged, drawing a large sigil on the floor in chalk.

"As the moon darkens, we transmute the old, to make way for the new. Removing harm, we release that which no longer serves us. We awaken our inner wisdom to clear the path toward alignment and transformation. So mote it be."

Once Hannah finished her intonation, she sat down as well, joining Ashlin. They placed a large, dark mirror on the floor between them. After the defeat of the Illusionix a few years ago, they regularly met to perform magick rituals correlated to the phases of the moon. On this night, as the full moon had passed, they focused on banishing evil powers and lessening the hold of nefarious forces, like the Dream Haunters. Hannah reached into a nearby jar, grabbed a handful of sand, and dusted it across the surface. Reaching their hands out to each other, they sat in silence, awaiting guidance from beyond.

They closed their eyes, their breath the only sound in the room besides the crackling of the wicks in the candles. The sweet smell of melted wax wafting past their noses.

"I feel a message is coming," Hannah said. "Remain still until it crosses over into this plane."

The sand began to slowly shake and move, ever so slightly, on the surface of the mirror. It was rearranging itself into fine letters.

"Now, open your eyes," Hannah said. She parted her eyelids and gazed into the mirror between them. They both leaned in.

"What does it say?" Ashlin asked excitedly. Upon the mirror was drawn a series of spirals in the sand, and in the middle was scrawled a verse:

Seven Moons
Seven Suns

Sisters of Skye
We are One
Hannah read it out loud as a howling wind began to shake the windowpanes. Then a second verse appeared:
I Separate but Also Allow
I Stand in Silence Until You Know How
With Just a Twist, Reveal the Unseen
Access the Timeline in Between
Before they could move, the spirals began to swirl and rearrange, this time spelling out a third verse. Ashlin began to read:
Seven Riddles Precede the Shadow Hour
Gather the Keys of our Legacy Power
Unlock the Crossroads under the Darkest Skies
Or Within This Room Meet Your Demise
The floorboards of the room began to creak and Hannah's heart started beating faster and faster. Then the wind violently broke through one of the small windows, slamming the swinging pane open and blowing out the candles.

Hannah and Ashlin jumped up in shock, startled and shrouded in darkness. Hands shaking, Hannah walked toward the window. The room glowed from the light of the waning moon.

Her thoughts raced. *Or Within This Room Meet Your Demise.* Who was going to meet their demise? Ashlin? Herself? They were the only ones who ever came up to the turret room. In fact, her Aunt Jewelia was the only other person who even knew it existed.

"Whose demise? One of us?" Ashlin stammered, attempting to help her with the window.

"Seven moons and seven suns...could that mean, seven days?"

"It's seven days until Samhain," Ashlin whispered.

Hannah stared at her in alarm. "If we don't solve the seven riddles and gather the keys in seven days, someone will meet their demise?" she croaked with trepidation.

"In this room?" Ashlin eyes scanned the bare walls.

"A warning...from beyond the veil. What will the keys unlock at the crossroads under darkest skies? Another dark force or our legacy? Our power?" she speculated, her thoughts spinning. "*Sisters of Skye*? As in, the Skye family? My family?"

Their eyes met as they turned from the window together, their thoughts syncing.

"My parents?" Hannah added in a whisper. She was half surprised to hear the words cross her lips into the air. Her mind had been filled with so much information that she could hardly contain it, her thoughts rushing as if she had been connected to a quantum runway—the wisdom channeling fast into her consciousness.

But when they returned to sit by the mirror, the spirals and messages were gone. Hannah stared into Ashlin's eyes searchingly. Had the time finally come where she would no longer be able to defeat the evil forces? The warning of someone's demise was pretty direct. She couldn't bear something happening to Ashlin, who had become such a good friend to her since she'd arrived in Maple Hollow years ago. Her heart ached at the thought of losing someone else she cared about. But Mercury retrograde was underway until November 10th, and ever since her battle with the Dream Haunters those first few weeks on the island, she knew what its overlap with Halloween could bring.

The two women extended their arms in the air and chanted phrases of magickal closing, sealing the sanctity of the circle and thanking those who had communicated with them.

Hannah took a deep breath, put her lips together, and, as if she were blowing out candles on a birthday cake, exhaled slowly across the mirror. The sand scattered into the air. She wished she could erase the thoughts from her mind, blow away that foreboding message of destruction, just as easily. But she could not.

A surge of anxiety raced through her blood. Fear of what was to come and doubt about her ability to stop it began to rise. The clock was now ticking toward the shadow hour, and it was up to her to gather the keys and, with a twist, reveal the unseen. Someone had one week left to live. She hoped it wasn't one of them.

Chapter Two

THE WHISPERING WHISKERS

October 25, 2013

Hannah sat up in her bed with a start, her heart pounding in her chest, struggling to fill her lungs with air. She had awoken from a nightmare, her body still reeling. The creeping hold of fear had taken over her limbs, her muscles tight and stiff with stress. Her neck throbbed and her hands were clinging to the bedsheets in tight fists. A thin layer of perspiration coated her forehead and behind her knees.

Midnight was curled up between her ankles, his black furry body burrowed into the blankets, his arm wrapped over his head covering his eyes. But as Hannah woke from her nap, he darted up in shock, springing into the air, and scampered out into the hallway, away from whatever danger might have precipitated her reaction.

In the dream, Hannah had been in a dark corridor that seemed to go on forever. Her lungs had contracted, suffocating her breath. The further she'd walked into the darkness of the hallway, the more she'd felt the presence of something pursuing her from behind. A woman's voice had reverberated within the passageway, which she could still hear echoing in her mind:

I Cannot Help but Run
Through the Channels I Churn
A Ladder I Descend
Darkness at Every Turn

This seemed different from the prophecy she and Ashlin had received the night before. The prophecy felt more like a personal instruction, but this reminded her of a guessing game, like the ancient riddle of the hourglass: *Two bodies have I, though both joined in one, the stiller I stand, the faster I run.* It had to be the first of the seven riddles the prophecy implied were coming.

Hannah grabbed for her dream journal and scribbled her fading memories on the pages as the paper struggled to turn, the adhesive clinging to the binding. The pen scratched on the page, its ink drying out from so many recordings of her otherworldly experiences.

She realized she was going to be late for work at the Whispering Whiskers Lounge—cat café by day, piano lounge by night. She'd tried to squeeze in the quick nap before her shift at six, given that she'd barely slept all night after receiving the prophecy. Not that insomnia was anything new to her lately. And now it was a quarter past five and there was just enough time to jump in the shower before heading out.

She hurried down the long upstairs hallway to the bathroom. It was adorned with flickering sconces, a claw-foot tub, and fluffy towels on iron hooks. She stepped into the separate shower stall, an addition her aunt had thankfully installed, and relaxed into the steaming water.

As she finished up, her eyes drifted to the drain, where there was a small ball of her hair gathered on the grate. She had noticed this happening more and more lately—first a few hairs, and now regularly a handful. She paused to wonder if this was normal, but then stepped out and promptly forgot all about it.

She quickly changed her clothes and grabbed her bag. As she made her way down the grand staircase of the manor, rain pounding against the windows and flashes of lightning ricocheting off the mirrors on the walls, Hannah decided her bike was out of the question and she would drive to town. She darted through the kitchen to the exterior garage. It was just a few steps off the back door, and there were plenty of cars to choose from. Old Man Adams, the caretaker of the manor, collected and restored cars as a hobby but rarely drove them. He had generously left the keys on hooks by the back door in case Jewelia or Hannah needed them. This was just one of the many ways he looked out for Hannah and her aunt. He was more like a family member than an employee, having raised Jewelia since she was a child.

Hannah jumped into the closest car, revved the engine to life, and began to drive down the winding road away from the manor, her headlights cutting through the low fog.

She loved thunderstorms. They were one of her favorite parts of nature. As she slowly made her way through the manor grounds, the auburn leaves of the tall maple trees waved at her departure. She navigated the twisty roadway to the iron gates that marked the edge of the estate. As her car approached the gates, embossed with the Skye family crest, they slowly opened, their metal creaking and scraping across the ground.

Soon she could see the glowing lamps of Maple Hollow lining the rain-washed streets, twinkling orange lights wrapped around the posts. The rain had chased everyone inside, and there was an energy and buzz spilling out of the restaurants she drove past; tourists from all over the world had descended on the tiny island to celebrate Halloween.

First, there would be a mystical Masquerade Ball at the historic Maple Hollow Theater, followed by several days of spooky festivities—corn mazes, hayrides, a farmer's market, apple-bobbing, bake sales, story-telling sessions, and metaphysical fair, to name just a few. Concluded by the town's traditional three-day "Halloween Hollow" festival, which this year included a special art exhibit, hosted by the Whispering Whiskers and a Silent Supper, hosted by Skye Manor—a celebration of Samhain and an opportunity to dine with the dead.

When Hannah arrived at work, the lounge was bustling and full—Friday nights were one of their busiest times. The atmosphere felt warm and inviting as she entered. Groups of people sat at small tables sipping cocktails and coffee, all the while visiting with the resident cats. Twin sister owners, Varlina and Delvina Lanuaria, split their time between the daytime café and evening lounge, respectively. Varlina had created the café as a sanctuary for cats, as she had always felt called to protect them. Eventually, she hired Wendy Airmeitha on as head chef, who made sure there was always an endless supply of pumpkin spice confections available for guests. Delvina, a pianist herself and burgeoning artist, used the lounge as her exhibit space, filling the walls with her cat-inspired paintings. Hannah played the piano for guests during the dinner hour several nights a week and helped with the cats occasionally during the day. It was the best of both worlds for her. She loved getting to interact with all the animals while not having to really socialize with the customers, unless someone requested a special song or came up to leave a tip in the fishbowl that sat atop the baby grand in the corner.

"She's been waiting for you," Varlina cooed as a striped tabby cat with white encircled eyes and cinnamon spice-colored patches down her back rubbed against Hannah's legs and paced around her.

"Aw, hello, Nutmeg," Hannah said, reaching down to stroke the tortoise shell tabby's fur. Nutmeg chirped a happy meow and arched her back to meet Hannah's hand, shaking her tail in excitement. She was one of her favorite cats from the lounge, and always came to greet her.

But by this time, nearly all the cats were happy to see her, as her first shift duty was to take care of feeding time. Hannah stepped behind the counter and grabbed the large container of cat food, doling out heaping scoops of kibble into a long row of cat bowls. The cats scurried and jockeyed for position, then hungrily began to crunch on their evening delights. Once they had gotten their fill, each cat casually returned to its favorite perch or cozy bed, to fastidiously clean up from the feast.

Hannah situated herself at the piano, reviewed her playlist for the night, and began to play. Before long, her fishbowl was filled with requests and the dinner hour flew by. Delvina emerged from the kitchen rolling a large cart filled with boxes.

"I'm afraid I can't stay for closing tonight. I have to run these plates and utensils over to the theater for the Masquerade Ball tomorrow. See you there!" Delvina announced, as she hurried past Hannah, still sitting at the piano.

"No problem," Hannah reassured her. "And I'm all set to open tomorrow, as well."

After the last patron checked out and all the wait staff departed, Hannah began to clean up for the night, carrying the dirty dishes back to the kitchen. She was aware that while her hands felt fine, her back felt weak after only playing for a few hours. This didn't use to happen. The slight pain extending across the middle of her back made her wince as she carried the stacks of plates. Maybe she was sitting wrong, she thought. She didn't always have the best posture, even though she tried to be cognizant of it.

There had been so many customers that night, the guests' dishes, including the cats' bowls, made a pile that was almost too large for the sink, stacked precariously on top of each other and teetering with each new one that was added. Inevitably, it took just one more mug to topple the whole pile. A large calamity ensued as the dishes crashed down onto the hard tile floor.

Hannah felt her face flush with frustration as she scrambled to catch a plate or two, but it was no use. She ended up crouched on the ground, picking up small pieces of ceramic, wincing as her knees pressed into the unforgiving floor. She tried her best to pick up all the pieces, but many had scattered under a tall hutch containing many of the appliances for the kitchen. She waved her arm underneath it to see if any stray pieces were there, and the opening of the spoon ring on her thumb caught on a small rope. She tugged her hand to release it, turning her wrist back and forth, and when that didn't work, bent down further for a closer look and reached underneath to untangle herself.

When her other hand met the rope, she traced its length and realized it was attached to the floor. After freeing her ring, Hannah rose to her feet and carefully removed each appliance, placing them on a large steel table in the middle of the kitchen. Curiosity quickened her pulse. Did the twins know about this?

Once the hutch was cleared, she carefully rocked it back and forth, moving it gradually to the side. It was then that she could fully see the rope and what it was attached to, and a slight chill crept across her skin. It was a square opening in the tile floor, covered with wood, with the rope attached like a handle. Hannah grabbed it and tugged on the door. When it opened, all she could see was a ladder descending into the darkness. Her mind immediately began to recite a line from the riddle in her dream, *A Ladder I Descend.* There was a trap door that led beneath the Whispering Whiskers. This suddenly reminded her of the one she had discovered under the rug in the library of Skye Manor, which led to the hidden spell room containing the *Grimoire de Skye.* Hannah had a flash of realization. What if her dream had been a premonition? What if this was the ladder she was meant to descend to solve the first riddle? She couldn't resist the urge to find out. Without further deliberation she decided...she was going in.

CHAPTER THREE

THE TUNNELS

Hannah's feet trembled as they navigated the corrugated metal steps of the ladder. It was surrounded by earthen walls, a stark contrast from the stone walls of the manor. When she reached the bottom, she grabbed a matchbook from the lounge out of her pocket—striking one until it burst into flame. She could see nothing more than narrow darkness in both directions, along with Nutmeg, who had skillfully followed her down and was trailing softly behind with trepidation and curiosity. There was a low, ominous wind. It undulated in its intensity, howling at times past her ringing ears.

The deeper Hannah explored, the louder the wind became. How could there be wind? Where was it blowing through...or to? She felt sure there must be another opening. But how far down did this passageway go? A sharp fear struck her heart, and her hands began to shake with adrenaline. Yet she had no choice but to face the riddle.

She began to walk further into the cavernous tunnel. It was deep within the earth, and the smell of soil permeated the walls. How had she never heard of a tunnel like this before? Hannah wondered if anyone else knew it existed. And if so, could that person be down here also at this very moment?

She noticed Nutmeg sniffing around and struck another match, illuminating the black, dank soil around her feet. There were small, loose stones strewn about. They almost appeared to be pieces of ice, clear and colorless. She bent over and picked up a few, putting them in her pocket.

Suddenly, she heard a loud smack above her head, and then the small clicking sound of a lock. Lunging back up the ladder, Hannah pressed her hands into the trap door. It did not budge. Had the wind slammed it shut? Was there someone on the other side? Or maybe Delvina returned to the lounge for some reason, saw the passageway exposed and locked the door, not realizing Hannah was within? Or did someone else lock it? Someone with a darker motive, intentionally trapping her in this dark tunnel?

Her stomach began to knot and seize. "Hello?" she croaked. Blood rushed to her head and her heart instantly began to pound like a racehorse when the gates fly open. "Help! Delvina?" she yelled, hoping someone would answer. She could hear the soft clicking of the other cats' claws as they paced around the tile floor above her.

"I'm in here!" she yelled again. But no one responded.

Hannah spun around as she began to hear a distant pounding. It seemed to come from deep within the earth, very far away, and set off an echo that rushed through the ground beneath her and within the walls: first, a thunderous boom, then a quick rushing sound. It set off a paralysis inside her. She couldn't decide which way to go. Both directions felt tenuous and un-certain. The tunnel was churning around her, like the riddle had foretold. She finally made a choice.

Not wanting to use up too many of her matches, Hannah had to feel rather than see her way, her hands fumbling along the subterranean walls bursting with craggy roots. As she proceeded down the long, dark hall, she realized that paths branched off it. It wasn't just one tunnel—it was a network, with multiple path-ways sprouting off the main one she was on. Some even had doors blocking the entrance. Others were obscured by the large cobwebs and scraggly roots that covered the dirt walls.

The wind sound increased and she began to feel a slight push from behind her. It was as if it was di-recting her forward, encouraging her. As she made progress further into the tunnel, she discovered a rusty lantern. Lighting it, she continued carefully forward, first cautiously and then with more curious vigor. She began to visualize in her mind the row of shops on the main street in town and wondered which building she might be underneath. Eventually she found herself breaking into a quick walk, then a slow jog, making the flames of the lantern waver and dance. Nutmeg, in tow, first pranced and then galloped alongside her.

As she forged ahead, her anxiety grew. She began to hear a rustling and panicked that there was someone behind her, down there with her. But the earth would be too soft to hear the echo of footsteps. She repeated the riddle in her mind:

I Cannot Help but Run
Through the Channels I Churn
A Ladder I Descend
Darkness at Every Turn

I cannot help but run? So, she did.

Hannah ran and ran, wondering how far the tunnels stretched. The island itself wasn't that big. Would she end up beneath the sea if she went too far?

The tunnel-scape began to change, and the air became thinner and thinner. Winded from running, Hannah stopped to catch her breath. It was as if the tunnel was competing with her for the air. The wind that had pushed her on had waned and she suddenly felt light-headed. As she stooped over, she lost her footing and collapsed onto the moist ground. Alone in the darkness of the tunnels, she felt her world go black.

Eventually she awoke with a gasp. It seemed like hours had passed, but it could have only been minutes. Time began to spiral around her as her confusion slowly dissolved. She had never fainted before, even though she'd been feeling dizzy lately. Hannah shuddered and quickly rose to her feet, fumbling for the lantern.

How long had she been down there? How far had she run? And how would she get out if she went back and the trap door in the lounge was still blocked?

As she shifted her gaze from her feet to the tunnel beyond, she noticed that the ceiling above her was now thickly full of roots. Then she saw a beam of light. It was white, shining against a wall farther down the tunnel. The roots seemed to undulate, almost as if they were pointing toward it.

As she moved closer, the light spread wider and brighter against the earthen floor. It was moonlight! And in its soft glimmer—an exit. The roots snaked up the wall toward the ray of light. Hannah's heart skipped a beat. Were these vines?

She began to run once again, hope in her heart. She could see a makeshift rope ladder, and she quickly grabbed Nutmeg. Holding her close, Hannah gingerly made her way up the ladder toward the opening.

When she got to the top, the moon shined down brightly into her eyes. A cool glow illuminated her face, bringing relief to her soul as she emerged from the darkness. To her total surprise, she was back at Skye Manor, surrounded by the large, orange pumpkins of the grand pumpkin patch. She must have traveled the whole length of the island, from the town to the manor, underground. The tunnels were a subterranean pathway that connected the two!

As she and Nutmeg stepped out into the pumpkin patch, Hannah remembered the profound recurring dream she used to have before coming to Maple Hollow: the mysterious pumpkin patch and the tingling, life-force connection she experienced as the vines spiraled up her legs. And then the power she'd felt in real life when awakening the vines to save her Aunt Jewelia and friend Madame Morgan. In fact, Hannah realized, the earthen hole she'd just climbed out of was similar to the one Jewelia and Morgan were trapped in during her first battle with the Dream Haunters, those forces of darkness that wanted nothing more than to entrap human souls within their nightmares.

Might there be other tunnel entrances, elsewhere in town or under the manor grounds? A combination of fear and fascination rose within Hannah. She had never before experienced the pumpkin patch from underneath. Yet it had come through for her once again. The vines had led her home.

CHAPTER FOUR

THE MANOR

Hannah ran toward the manor, looking for anyone to talk to about the tunnels. The first person she saw was Old Man Adams.

"Hey!" she yelled as soon as she saw him crossing the lawn.

"Hannah? I thought you were at work! Are you okay?" he asked, bewildered.

"I was at the lounge closing up when I found a passageway under the kitchen. It led us here!"

"Us? What do you mean?"

"It's underground. It runs beneath the town. I nearly got lost in it with Nutmeg"—she gestured to the cat, who was exploring her new environment—"but then I followed the roots of the pumpkin patch and realized I'd made it all the way to the manor."

"An underground passage!" Old Man Adams exclaimed in surprise. "In our pumpkin patch?" he added, even more surprised. "You mean the hole your aunt and Morgan were trapped in? I certainly didn't realize it led anywhere," Adams admitted. "So, wait—why did you go through the tunnel?"

"After I went down into it, I was trapped," Hannah continued hastily. "I tried to escape, but I was locked in, so I had no choice but to follow where the tunnel went, which is how I ended up here. I heard noises when I was underground," she added. "I think someone else may have been down there."

Adams raised his eyebrows.

"Tunnel?" They were interrupted by the sound of Jewelia Skye's voice as she appeared around the corner of the manor. Often when she was restless, she went out for walks in the moonlight. Her long, shiny black hair was illuminated as it peaked out of the corners of her hood. She wore an ankle-length satin nightgown, obscured by her heavy dark cloak. "Are you okay, love?" she asked Hannah with concern.

"Jewelia!" Hannah felt relieved to see her aunt. "Yes, there's a tunnel."

Jewelia's eyes widened, and then scanned the grounds as she considered this information. "I have heard lore of tunnels on this island for many years, but no one has ever found them ... until now," she mused. "How did you find it?"

"I was closing up for the night at work and had an accident in the kitchen with the dishes. When I went to clean it up, I found a trap door. I couldn't resist checking it out." Hannah made a mental note to herself to ask Jewelia about the riddle. "Once I got down into the tunnel, I noticed there was a wind."

"A wind?" Old Man Adams echoed, confused. "How can there be wind underground?"

Jewelia raised an eyebrow as if she had some idea. "Did the roots lead you back?" she asked knowingly.

Hannah scooped up Nutmeg. "Yes. I followed them, and they led me here."

"Ah, the network of roots will always lead you back to yourself," Jewelia said knowingly.

"But I'm pretty sure there was someone there in the tunnel," Hannah said again. "Someone trapped me!" she declared with an edge of fear.

"Maybe it was Delvina," Old Man Adams said, inserting reason. "Maybe she just closed it to tidy up, not realizing you were inside."

"No, she'd left for the night, and she asked me to close up," Hannah said in protest. "But I did yell, and no one answered, so I had no choice but to keep going."

"Perhaps you were meant to," Jewelia said, winking.

"Thankfully, I'm opening tomorrow. I want to finish cleaning up before anyone gets there. But I'm a little afraid to go there myself after what happened. Will you go with me in the morning?" she asked Old Man Adams.

"Of course, little lady. Just come knock on my door when you're ready and I'll drive you over there. Will be good to have a look around," he said, patting her shoulder. "Come now, let's get you some tea." He put his arm around Hannah and the three of them walked toward his cabin near the edge of the woods. The air was filled with a symphony of the sea gently undulating in the background, mixed with the night song of crickets and the gentle coo of owls nestled in the trees.

Jewelia helped Adams prepare some warm water and then joined them at the table with three cups and a tin of chamomile teabags.

"There, there, dear, this should calm your nerves," she said, pouring the steaming liquid into her cup. "You've made a great discovery." She looked at Hannah with excitement. "I can only conclude that you were meant to find the passageway at this specific point in time."

Hannah slowing stirred her tea in a spiraling motion, her nerves starting to relax from the herbal aroma. "But why? It was terrifying. I'm sure I was trapped by someone," she repeated.

"Your fear is understandable," Jewelia assured her. "But now you are safe here at the manor. You found your way home and that's all that matters."

"I had a dream..." Hannah began.

"Yes, love?" Her aunt leaned in.

Hannah took the simplest approach to explaining it. "I heard a riddle. It seemed to be saying I should go into the tunnel."

"Do you remember it?"

"Yes. It said:

I Cannot Help but Run
Through the Channels I Churn
A Ladder I Descend
Darkness at Every Turn

"Ah, a descent into darkness," Jewelia said as she sipped her tea.

"When I was down there, it was like the earth was alive. I heard this boom and a rushing sound. I ran for a while, but I started to run out of air. Then I fell asleep—or passed out, I can't be sure."

"How interesting that it led you to the pumpkin patch." Jewelia drummed her fingers across her chin in contemplation.

"I'm going to keep a close eye on that hole," Old Man Adams assured them. "And I'll put a grate back over it, too, to make sure no one falls in!"

Hannah sat back in her chair and let the chamomile do its work. Tomorrow, she would have to ask Varlina and Delvina if either of them had come back to the lounge at closing time. She debated in her mind whether she should reveal the tunnel or not to them. It was, after all, connected to their place of business. They should know. But part of her wanted to investigate more first. As her fear subsided, her curiosity grew about where else the tunnels might lead, and who or what else might be down there.

Hannah and Jewelia finished their tea, left the cabin, and headed back to the manor, Nutmeg in tow. Hannah would return the cat to the lounge in the morning, but for now she needed rest.

Before she went to bed that night, she placed the small stones from the tunnel on her bedside table. They were beautiful and made her feel comforted, one of the few positive outcomes of that adventure. The starlight in the dark sky streamed through her window as she replayed the vision of the tunnels in her mind. Hannah still felt uneasy about losing consciousness underground. *Who had been down there with her and what did they want?* She fell into a deep sleep.

***

She found herself standing outside a colossal library, its towering architecture rivaling that of the Roman coliseum. She walked into the courtyard, massive columns towering high above her. In her mind, Hannah heard a woman's voice:
A Closed Hand Cannot Receive
A Distrusting Heart Cannot Relieve

The scene then quickly switched to a forest. In her hand was a remote control. Suddenly Hannah had a realization: she was, in fact, dreaming! Her conscious mind attaining a state of lucidity, she became innately aware of her dream world and her existence within it. Excited, she decided to press a button on the remote. And when she did, she was able to elevate her body into the air. The higher she rose, the more the landscape below her was revealed. It was the most amazing, breathtaking scene she had ever seen. A lush green valley expanded before her, crowned by a village and dotted with lakes, little houses, and endless trees. It was beyond beautiful, and it induced a feeling of awe and empowerment inside Hannah's heart.

Observing this scene, Hannah's curiosity rose about what was behind her. She then made another conscious decision to spin around in the air. But once she did, she was greeted by a brooding, dark, stormy sky filled with heavy gray clouds and an ominous darkness.

She then heard the voice again:

Spun Within the Salty Tide

The Soul's Song Cannot Be Denied

She turned once more to the verdant valley behind her; it was still there, gleaming in the breathtaking, golden sunlight. Then she awoke.

CHAPTER FIVE

THE SISTERS

OCTOBER 26, 2013

As Hannah entered the liminal state on her way back to the waking world, she tried to stay still and jog her memory. When the message began to reformulate in her mind, she grabbed her dream journal and scrawled the riddle quickly onto the page:

A Closed Hand Cannot Receive
A Distrusting Heart Cannot Relieve
Spun Within the Salty Tide
The Soul's Song Cannot Be Denied

Upon writing the last words, Hannah sat in reflection, petting Nutmeg curled up next to her; Midnight, displaced for the night, had gone to sleep with Jewelia. She realized that not only had she become lucidly aware in her dream, but the communications to her subconscious from the mysterious messenger were becoming more profound.

There had been an ominous storm brewing in the beyond, and the new riddle weighed heavily on her mind. *Who was closed, distrusting? Was it she herself who could not receive, or relieve? What was meant by the soul's song?* Then Hannah remembered she had to get up and get ready to open the lounge.

She promptly headed downstairs for breakfast. Jewelia and Wendy were scurrying about, filling the large kitchen with the comforting sounds of cooking. In the years since she'd returned to Maple Hollow, Wendy had perfected and expanded her culinary magick, taking on the chef role at the Whispering Whiskers as well as managing the menu at Skye Manor.

"Good morning, love," Jewelia chirped as Hannah entered.

"Good morning," Hannah said as she pulled out a chair and made herself cozy at the table.

"My goodness, you're looking a bit haggard, my dear!" Wendy raised an eyebrow at Hannah.

"Yes, I was late coming in." Hannah and Jewelia exchanged a glance. "The strangest thing happened to me at work. I found a tunnel underneath the lounge...it led me back here."

"Tunnel?" Wendy exclaimed.

"I think it's a whole network of tunnels. I received a message in my dream that really spurred me on to explore it," Hannah began, and recounted the whole story. "And by the way, meet Nutmeg," she added as the sound of cat nails prancing on the stone floor perked up everyone's ears. "She's from the lounge. She followed me into the passageway."

"Well, hello, Nutmeg," Wendy said, reaching out to gently scratch the cat's neck and ears. Nutmeg then proceeded to jump up on one of the side tables and make herself at home.

"Isn't it curious that you discovered the tunnel now?" Jewelia mused.

"There must be a significance," Wendy chimed in.

"Well, Ashlin and I did receive a communication, a prophecy really, the other night at our ritual," Hannah said. Finally, she had a chance to go into the details and hear Jewelia's thoughts. She knew it would make her feel so much better.

"What did it say?" her aunt asked. She normally didn't demand details about Hannah's magickal activities, but now that she was aware of a secret tunnel that led right to their dwelling, it made sense for her to be more concerned.

Hannah started reciting the prophecy:

Seven Moons
Seven Suns
Sisters of Skye
We are One

She hesitated for a moment, trying to remember more of it:

Seven Riddles Precede the Shadow Hour
Gather the Keys of our Legacy Power
Unlock the Crossroads under the Darkest Skies
Or Within This Room Meet Your Demise

Jewelia and Wendy's eyes became wide. "Sisters of Skye!" Jewelia said out loud.

"Demise?" Wendy blurted.

"We're the sisters, right?" Hannah asked. "I mean, we're not really sisters, although our family name is Skye."

Jewelia paused in reflection. "The Seven Sisters," she finally said, a faraway look in her eye. "It can't be," she scoffed, shifting her breakfast dishes in dismissal.

"What?" Wendy stared, expressionless, at Jewelia.

"There is a legend about seven women who lived on the Isle of Skye—our ancestors," she began as Wendy leaned in. "Suspected as members of a coven of witches, they were persecuted for their beliefs and they fled the island, coming here to establish Maple Hollow."

"Yes, Ashlin told me about the families coming over," Hannah affirmed. "But I thought the women were friends and fellow healers, not sisters?"

"We don't know much of the details," Jewelia replied. "But yes, despite what many think, the Seven Sisters weren't related to each other."

"Right," Hannah said. "And that's why you and I have different powers than Morgan, Wendy, and Ashlin. We carry on our own legacies."

"Yes. They were called sisters because they were so connected," Jewelia continued. "Once they came here, they established new identities, but vowed to never forget their origins. One of the Seven Sisters took on the name of their homeland. That is how we became the Skye family."

Hannah couldn't believe that she hadn't ever heard about this. She knew her ancestors had fled their home and come to the island of Maple Hollow to live in peace, but she didn't know these details.

Then she remembered the other part of the prophecy, and quickly recited it for Jewelia and Wendy:

I Separate but Also Allow

I Stand in Silence Until You Know How

With Just a Twist, Reveal the Unseen

Access the Timeline in Between

Wendy grabbed a pen to write down the phrases for closer examination. "That's intriguing. Let's start with the first line. What separates but also allows?"

"Maybe like a net? A fishing net that has holes for water to pass through?" Jewelia mused.

"Okay, maybe. What stands in silence?" Hannah asked.

"A statue? A tree?" Wendy began brainstorming, spouting off possibilities.

Hannah gave her an inquisitive look, feeling hesitation but entertaining the options.

"What is twisted to reveal the unseen?" Wendy said, biting the top of her pen.

"A curtain!" Hannah answered confidently.

"Hmm, that's not a bad one." Wendy bent her neck to one side.

"The timeline in between, I like that. But in between what?" Jewelia asked.

"The seen and the unseen?" Hannah offered.

"Perhaps. Then there is the crossroads that appears at the shadow hour." Wendy underlined the words.

"Could the shadow hour be the new moon, or maybe an eclipse?" Hannah wondered, looking up at them.

"Oh yes, it could be one of those. I mean technically, all hours have shadow," Jewelia remarked.

"That's true," Wendy said, with a look of doubt.

"And the crossroads?" Hannah said. "That could be literal or metaphorical. A transition in life, an actual intersection of streets, a turning point?"

"Right, there are a lot of options with that one." Jewelia ran her finger across her chin in contemplation.

"Ashlin said she thought the seven moons and seven suns could mean seven days."

"Oh, yes, that's good, seven days. Seven keys?"

"Maybe. But I can't figure out what the keys are. I'm not sure which ones it might be referring to, since there are so many in the great hall."

"What if it doesn't mean those keys?" Jewelia said with a wry look.

Hannah paused, thinking about the riddles she'd received in her dreams. "And there was another," she shared.

"Another dream message?" Wendy asked.

"Tell me everything," Jewelia said, more serious now.

"Well, the first one, as you know, led me down into the tunnel, the descent into darkness and all that. This one came to me just as I woke up this morning." She cleared her throat and spoke slowly:

A Closed Hand Cannot Receive
A Distrusting Heart Cannot Relieve
Spun Within the Salty Tide
The Soul's Song Cannot Be Denied

"The salty tide? Hmm, that's interesting." Wendy reached for the spices she'd used for breakfast, examining the labels. "Salt is often used for cleansing and protection. In fact, each herb and spice in my cupboard has a special property that can be called upon depending on the situation. And let's see, salty tide...tide can represent both renewal and loss, since a tide gives and takes, ebbs and flows, comes and goes. Of course, the tide is created by the moon."

"Oh, you're right, I hadn't thought of that," Hannah said, leaning on the table with her elbows.

"The soul's song...could this be related to music?" Jewelia offered, deep in thought.

They were silent for a moment. The mention of music got Hannah thinking about playing piano, which reminded her that she needed to get to the Whispering Whiskers.

"I should take Nutmeg back and clean up the lounge. I'm opening today, since Varlina is helping Delvina set up at the Masquerade Ball. I need to ask them about the tunnels. Maybe they know something."

Hannah finished up her breakfast and made her way, with Nutmeg, out into the morning air. They met up with Old Man Adams at his cabin and he drove them into town. The bright golden and red leaves of the trees cascaded down as their car exited the manor grounds.

They arrived with just enough time to spare before the first customers arrived. Hannah fed the cats, who swarmed Nutmeg to sniff out her adventures. Old Man Adams helped her clean up the kitchen and secured the lock on the trap door. No one would be going in, or coming out—or so they thought.

CHAPTER SIX

THE DIS-EASE

It was the night of the Maple Hollow Masquerade Ball, and everyone was going. Hannah had asked Ashlin to meet for drinks beforehand. She needed her friend's insights into everything that had happened since the ritual. As the town librarian, Ashlin had a wealth of knowledge at her fingertips. She expected to see Varlina and Delvina at the ball, so she would ask them about the tunnel then. She really needed to know who shut the trap door on her. And if it wasn't one of them, were they okay? As she wondered, her anxiety rose about the events of the night before.

She took a slow walk to town, her costume tucked into her bag, saving her energy for the ball later. This would be her seventh Halloween Hollow, and just like every other year, she enjoyed the flurry of tourists and locals filling the streets. Cascading fall leaves crunched beneath people's feet as they scurried between the various shops doing last-minute shopping for the ball. Halloween was her favorite holiday. She paused to admire the spooky decorations in each shop window. Some were whimsical, with bats and cats, while others were darker, with skulls and ravens. In one window, she saw a row of ghostly paper streamers hanging side by side, their white bodies narrowing into long curly spirals. This reminded her of the spirals in the sand that had appeared on the mirror. The Seven Sisters had tried to warn her about a potential demise...but what did that mean? And why now?

She made her way to a small wine bar near the Maple Hollow Theater and stepped inside, grabbing a private table in the corner. Shortly afterward, before even being greeted by a server, she heard the tinkle of a bell announcing a new patron's arrival. Her eyes lifted and she smiled when she saw Ashlin standing at the entrance, looking straight at her.

She waved. "Hey!" reaching out to hug Ashlin in a warm welcome.

"I love the glitter!" Ashlin exclaimed, remarking on Hannah's sparkling cheeks. She settled down in her chair.

"Aw, thanks." Hannah felt a blush warming her face. "My costume is in here." She patted her bag.

"Can I get you anything?" a waitress asked, looking at Ashlin.

"I'll have a glass of white wine, thanks." Ashlin said, closing the small menu without perusing it.

"Same," Hannah said, smiling back at the waitress.

"So, hey, what's going on? You sounded a bit off on the phone earlier." Ashlin reached her hand across the table to Hannah's. "Have you been wracking your brain about that prophecy? I have."

"Yes, but things are getting more complicated. Last night, I was closing the lounge and found a secret tunnel under the island."

"You what?" Ashlin inhaled sharply and began coughing.

"It was through a trap door in the floor of the kitchen," Hannah explained. "I felt like someone might have been down there with me. Well, besides Nutmeg—she followed me down. I ended up back at the manor, since the tunnel led underground all the way to the pumpkin patch."

"The pumpkin patch?" Ashlin exclaimed. She looked concerned, then frustrated. "Why, as the keeper of the wisdom of the island, have I never heard of this tunnel?"

"I was hoping you had. Jewelia has heard rumors of tunnels, but no one else seems to know anything," Hannah replied, disappointed.

Ashlin dropped her head to one side. "Are you okay?"

The waitress arrived with their wine and a bowl of honey-roasted hazelnuts. Hannah took a sip and began picking at the snack. "I haven't been feeling myself lately. Worrying about the prophecy and who might have been in the tunnels seems to be making things worse. I guess the good thing is, I'm having lucid dreams and received some of the seven riddles the prophecy talked about."

"You have?" Ashlin asked, surprised.

"Yeah, from a voice in my dreams. These riddles are like rhyming messages. I'm not entirely sure what they mean. But the first one is why I went down into the tunnels. It said:

I Cannot Help but Run
Through the Channels I Churn
A Ladder I Descend
Darkness at Every Turn

And then this morning, I received another one:

A Closed Hand Cannot Receive

A Distrusting Heart Cannot Relieve
Spun Within the Salty Tide
The Soul's Song Cannot Be Denied

"Hmm, through the channels I churn..." Ashlin trailed off, in deep thought. "Closed hand, distrusting heart...receipt, relief..." She swirled the wine around in her glass. "Spun within the salty tide...is that like cotton candy or saltwater taffy? Soul's song...like the Masquerade Ball tonight?"

"I guess it could be. If I felt better, I might be able to figure more things out!"

"Tell me more about what's wrong," Ashlin asked, her curiosity piquing.

"Well, it's gradually been building up over quite some time. I've noticed a lot of little things. I guess I just ignored it before." Hannah felt deflated. "Things like my vision has been doing weird things, and sometimes I get dizzy for no reason. My back has been hurting after I play the piano, which it never used to. I feel tired all the time, and sometimes it feels like it's hard for me to catch my breath. Like the air is being squeezed out of my lungs," she added, exasperated. "I mean, I still can do everything I normally do, but I just don't feel as sharp as I should."

"Have you been sleeping?" Ashlin asked with concern.

"Sort of. Sometimes I've had total insomnia and just stay up all night thinking, wishing I could fall asleep. I get super cold, like unreasonably cold, and I've noticed lately that I'm losing more of my hair than usual. I also keep getting this annoying twitch in my left eye. It drives me crazy! Maybe it's from lack of sleep?"

"Ah, symptoms of a dis-ease," Ashlin said empathetically.

"You mean I have a disease?" Hannah was confused.

"Sort of. The concept is that all ailments are physical expressions of a greater unease at the spiritual and emotional level."

"That makes sense. Sometimes I feel like I'm just not with it, like I'm in a fog, but a mental one. In your research, have you ever read about these symptoms? Do you have any idea what might be causing them?" she asked, suddenly optimistic that her friend might hold the answers. Ashlin could commune with books, after all, absorbing the information directly from the author without ever opening it. Hannah had been practicing this skill, and it had rapidly improved her ability to obtain vast amounts of knowledge on whatever subject she desired. Still, Ashlin could commune at a much faster rate.

"I do have an idea of what it could be, but I'd need to check into a few things," Ashlin replied. "When is your next shift at the lounge?"

"I'm playing tomorrow night."

"Okay, then give me till tomorrow. I'll see what I can find."

"Great, thanks," Hannah said, looking searchingly into Ashlin's eyes.

"Anything for you. It might be what helps unravel all these strange clues you keep receiving," Ashlin said, taking a sip of her drink.

Hannah was glad she had confided in her about feeling out of sorts. She didn't want to suffer alone anymore. She hadn't said anything about her symptoms to Old Man Adams, Jewelia, or Morgan. She didn't want them to be concerned. But she was beginning to worry herself and was not sure where to turn. She felt slightly hopeful that maybe it really was all part of the larger challenge of the prophecy, and maybe Ashlin could help her figure it out.

"I can't wait to see what Wendy has cooked up for the ball tonight," she said, changing the subject.

"Maybe there will be something salty!" Ashlin said wryly as they emptied their drinks and snatched the last nuts from the bowl.

CHAPTER SEVEN

THE BALL

Hannah and Ashlin stepped into the ballroom of the grand Maple Hollow Theater. It was one of the most magnificent buildings in town, ornate both inside and out. Twinkling flames flickered from candelabras affixed to the dark-paneled walls on either side. Thin, luminous fabric arched over the ceiling, cascading down across the open air. Heavy, dark metal chandeliers hung between the gathered fabric. A low fog crept across the ground, obscuring everyone's feet, making them look as if they were floating. Sparkling fireflies filled the dark and mysterious air, making it glisten.

A string quartet sat on chairs in a corner, serenading the partygoers with a delightfully spooky waltz. Everyone was decked out in the most elaborate costumes Hannah had ever seen. And cats from the lounge had made their home at the theater for the night as well, including Nutmeg. They snuck under women's hoop skirts, chased each other across the dance floor, and perched upon the railings, observing everyone from above. Some of the women's dresses had small jewels that reflected the candle flames, glowing in the dark.

Their long skirts swished along the floor, swirling as they swept by. A deep purple glow filled the room, with bright orange spotlights swooping about.

Every guest had donned an ornate masquerade mask, obscuring their identity. Some of the masks were bordered by shiny cords, some had glitter patterns upon them, and others had various feathers and beads attached. The room was so dark that some guests appeared to have no eyes at all, the gaping holes of their mask showing only vast darkness where their eyes should be.

At the far end of the room was a grand fireplace, within which was a roaring fire. The peaks of the flames reached up the chimney, turning into sparkling embers, then disappearing. The flames reflected in the carved ice sculptures that were placed about on tall circular tables covered with long black tablecloths. Laughter and chatter filled the room as guests welcomed each other, gossiped, and shared small exchanges.

Hannah had carefully curated her costume for the event. This year, she was embodying her favorite instrument—the piano. It wasn't just her current profession; it also signified her connection to Wixby and her discovery of the healing power of sound frequency. She seemed to have a talent for curating different fabrics, jewelry, wigs, and accessories. On her feet, she wore stunning Victorian-shaped, knee-high platform black boots with large, silver buckles wrapped in portable fairy light strips, seven times around each leg. The glow made her calves shimmer like a star-studded piano in the sky, and illuminated her path as she walked. Chunky block heels, that made her at least five inches taller, rose from the back. Above that, she wore a black, satiny waterfall skirt, which featured a border of white and black piano keys that cascaded down from the high to low hem. It was paired with a shapely black corset with shoulder straps, the front closure buckles matching her edgy boots.

Even the tiny details mattered. She had sewn into the corset loops small treble clef silver charms—a homage to her family crest. From the bottom buckle, hung the heavy iron skeleton keys to the manor Old Man Adams had given her. Around her neck, was the silver key necklace her aunt had gifted her, and from her ears hung long silver keys, hanging from French hooks. Her fingernails were painted alternating white and black, with treble clef decals on each, while her hands were adorned by piano key fingerless gloves that fit snuggly up over her elbows. Her wavy reddish hair was concealed by a black wig with long, flowing curls and blunt bangs, topped off by shoulder-length pigtails, one black and one white. She even had procured a cute piano-themed shoulder bag and a glittery eye mask with a sheet music design, to finish off the outfit.

She loved to hide hidden meaning in the costumes she put together. There was always something extra, another layer to everything she did. She felt this made the outfit so much more significant, interesting, and mysterious. A puzzle for others to solve in search of the true meaning.

She knew that, in general, most people created costumes by adapting the look of characters from popular movies, tv shows, or games. But for her, it involved so much more than that. The costumes were reflections of her soul, her existence throughout the ages. It was as if each one she selected was a version of herself that had or did exist somewhere in time, in another dimension. She never understood when people would choose to represent something they'd never want to be, or something as a gag joke, or something so dark and nefarious it could destroy them. The energy wasn't a match; it wasn't what she wanted to put out in the world.

When she had the opportunity to envision herself as something else, her imagination offered so many opportunities. Things that mattered to her. It's not to say her costumes weren't whimsical, since sometimes they could be, but the point was they held significance. They were timestamps of her life, guideposts on her journey, echoes of her existence.

Hannah and Ashlin had arrived a bit late, and the ball was already well underway. Upon arrival, Ashlin was quickly whisked away by co-workers from the library, pressing for her attention. Hannah scanned the room for Delvina and Varlina. It was easy to spot them, standing near the appetizers in their matching, elaborate, dark red ball gowns. The twins were truly identical except for their hair. Delvina's long, shiny, chestnut hair was pulled back into a decorative bun, while Varlina wore a long fiery red wig, the subtle waves cascading across her shoulders. They each had the same long noses, captivating eyes, and welcoming smiles, made all the more pronounced by their fantastical masks.

Delvina, always eager to taste-test the catering, was nibbling on one of the appetizers—which made sense, given that Whispering Whiskers was the sponsor of the event and she had meticulously planned the elaborate spread of food with Wendy, the culinary genius of Maple Hollow. Varlina, always ready for a cocktail, held a slim champagne glass in her right hand, her glittery clutch in the other.

"Ah, I've found you two!" Hannah said as she approached the sisters.

"So much for my disguise," Varlina replied sarcastically with a smile.

"Hannah, you look lovely." Delvina held out her arms for a hug.

"Thank you," Hannah said graciously, anxious to get past the small talk. "Were either of you at the lounge late last night, just after closing time?"

Delvina stopped in the middle of her chewing. "Not me. I left early, remember?" She looked at her sister. "Were you there?"

"No, why?" Varlina took another sip of her champagne.

"I...found something under the kitchen, under..." Hannah began with some hesitation.

"Under?" Varlina prompted, barely swallowing.

"I was cleaning up for the night, and in my haste, I had a little accident with the dishes." Hannah tried to down play what had happened, embarrassed by her clumsiness. She quickly followed with more explanation. "You know that really tall shelf with all the small appliances? I had to move it to clean up, and when I did...I found a trap door in the floor."

"A trap door?!" Varlina's eyes widened and Delvina stepped closer to hear Hannah over the music. "I've never noticed that."

"I couldn't help but check it out, and when I went in, Nutmeg followed me—curiosity, you know."

They both leaned in further with anticipation.

"But once I went down into the hole, the trap door closed behind me! I yelled, but no one answered. I thought maybe one of you had come back to help close up and might have accidentally shut me in."

Silence fell between them as the sisters shook their heads.

"My word, Hannah, are you okay?" Delvina set down her plate and reached for Hannah in consolation. "We were both at home all night, preparing our costumes," she said, passing her hands over the elaborate beadwork they had painstakingly sewed into silky fabric.

"We most certainly were not at the lounge last night," Varlina reiterated.

"If it wasn't us...who could have closed the trap door?" Delvina asked, scanning the room filled with masked guests. "And how did you get out if it was locked?" was her logical follow-up.

"I ended up taking the passageway all the way back to the manor, underground."

"Passageway?!" Varlina's eyes became wide.

"Yes. Apparently, there are underground tunnels all across the island. You didn't know about them?" Hannah asked.

Varlina looked at Delvina. A look of shock crossed both their faces as they sought to confirm their shared obliviousness about the trap door and the tunnels.

"No, certainly not," Varlina finally said in confirmation. "I've never heard of this!"

"So, this whole time, there's been a passageway under our lounge," Delvina murmured with both curiosity and concern.

"But there's something else," Hannah said with hesitation. "I wasn't alone in the tunnels."

"Yes, Nutmeg, always a curious one," Varlina remarked.

"No, someone besides Nutmeg. I never saw anyone, but I could feel they were there. I was being followed, chased even. I ran deep into the tunnels, not knowing where I was going. I think I might have even fainted. Then I saw the light of the moon above the manor grounds shining down. I was so relieved to have found a way out."

Varlina put her arm around Hannah. "You poor thing!"

"Who would be lurking below Maple Hollow? And why?" Delvina mused, her eyes searching the room around them.

CHAPTER EIGHT

THE TASTING

Hannah stepped behind the tables to see Wendy, who had been working on catering for the Masquerade Ball for most of the month of October. She knew she had been preparing extremely special concoctions and couldn't wait to see and taste the final products.

"Well, hello, Hannah! Don't you look lovely this evening, and so appropriate, I might add," Wendy said as Hannah moved closer.

"Aw, thanks. And same to you," Hannah reached out to hug her. Wendy's hair, which cascaded down around her ears towards her shoulders in gentle waves, was pulled back from her forehead with tiny barrettes attached to a botanical crown of greenery. She wore matching silver jewelry and a mid-length, flowy, burnt-out velvet dress with cascading fringe that fell around her calves, finished off with shiny black boots. Sewn throughout the fabric were dried herbs and flowers she had carefully handpicked from the manor's gardens and forest.

"I'm in awe at your amazing spread!" Hannah declared, gazing at the multiple tables filled with an array of appetizers.

"Thank you. I have so many things to show you! Based on that salty tide riddle you received in your dream, I've added some very special spice and salt combinations. There are seven courses in total."

"Seven?" Hannah immediately thought about the message of Seven Sisters, seven suns, seven moons. "What are they?"

"Here, let me move this one, I'm not sure where that came from." Wendy removed a silver tray from the table as she passed Hannah a small menu. Hannah quickly looked it over. "First, you should start with an amuse-bouche," Wendy continued.

"What's that?" Hannah was unsure of the phrase. She folded the menu and tucked it into her pocket.

"It's basically a little something to amuse the mouth, get the juices flowing, as it were." Wendy handed her a small spoon. It contained a thin slice of apple, garnished with pickled ginger and topped with a cinnamon stick.

"Apple, one of my favorites!" Hannah exclaimed. The smell of the spice wafted under her nose as she quickly crunched into the crisp slice. "What a modern twist on apple bobbing. I love it!" she remarked, thinking back to all the times as a child that she took part in the age-old tradition.

"And much easier than apple bobbing, I might add," Wendy said, smiling and passing another dish to Hannah. This one consisted of a small bowl with a spoon, upon which sat diced cubes of roasted winter squash and finely chopped tender beets, topped with a dusting of maple-sugared pecan crumble.

"Oh, warm autumn salad, yes! I love this combination."

"Madame?" a man's voice said, from behind Hannah. She spun around to see a tall gentleman, in a formal butler suit, holding a serving tray with a fluted, sparkling glass on it. "Compliments of the gentlemen," he said with a slight bow, turning his head to reference a tall man standing across the ballroom in a long, black cloak and chained metal mask that obscured his eyes.

"Oh, thank you," Hannah said with some confusion, and a bit of hesitation. But before she could catch a glimpse of him, or take a sip, he faded into the crowd and Wendy passed her another small plate. On it was a small slice of crusty rosemary bruschetta slathered in a creamy cashew cheese, topped with glowing cranberries, pomegranates, and figs, and crowned with a sprig of sage. Next to it was a small shot glass filled with dark orange liquid.

Hannah set the champagne down on the table so she could focus on the next course. "Now this is delicious," she said as she gobbled up the shiny fruit topping and crunched away. "What a wonderful flavor combination! And this?" She held up the shot glass.

"It's acorn soup," Wendy explained.

"So seasonal! Of course." Hannah quickly drank up the savory liquid, its warmth spreading from her throat to her chest.

"And now the palate cleanser." Wendy passed her another small spoon, upon which was a round dollop of light-yellow sorbet.

"Pear?" Hannah asked as she took a small taste.

"Exactly, with a hit of cardamom and clove," Wendy said, reaching for the next plate and waiting. "Here you go!" She handed Hannah a small, carved out mini-pumpkin filled with a steamy, thick liquid.

"I know what this is," Hannah said with excitement.

"And you would be right," Wendy said without surprise. "Pumpkin soup!" they both said together, smiling.

Hannah finished the soup off almost immediately, since it was one of her favorite things.

"Are you ready for the sweet stuff?" Wendy asked, handing Hannah a small, square plate.

"Always!"

"I know you're going to love this." Wendy produced a small stick of wood, through which were pierced three round balls of sugary dough.

"Donut holes? You didn't!" Hannah said with delight as she began to detach each small dough ball from the stick. Warm, soft, and extremely fresh, they seemed to melt in her mouth.

"Yes, spiked with nutmeg and allspice," Wendy said, smiling.

"Nutmeg?" Hannah was jolted out of her food coma, suddenly remembering the underground tunnels.

"There's one last thing." Wendy passed her a miniature mug with a tiny handle.

"What could top that?" Hannah wondered if they'd reached the end of the courses.

"Salted caramel chai!" Wendy smiled.

"You really are a culinary genius," Hannah said fervently, sipping the steamy, sweet liquid from the tiny mug.

"Thank you so much. I appreciate that." Wendy beamed, pleased her inventions were well received. "Let me know if you need anything. I'll be here late tonight cleaning up."

"Okay, thanks!" Hannah turned to look around the large ballroom as Wendy bustled away. The song had ended and loud clapping erupted from the crowd. The sugar from the delicious appetizers was beginning to course in her veins and revive memories of Halloweens past. Then, a hush fell over the room, and everyone's attention turned to Jewelia and Morgan. They were walking toward a raised podium on the stage to address the crowd.

CHAPTER NINE
THE WATCHER

"Welcome, everyone!" Jewelia began. The spotlight revealed her eye-catching off-shoulder black lace gown, the curved seams complimenting her shape. Her elaborately long bat sleeves and elegant mermaid train, cast long eerie shadows behind her. On her head, she wore a stunning halo headpiece embellished with crescent moons. "We are so thrilled to have you all gathered here today, to celebrate this most sacred of times in Maple Hollow."

Morgan chimed in. "As we usher in this darker time and turn the wheel of the year, we celebrate the bounty of the harvest." Dressed as a woodland queen; her forest green hoop skirt gown was embroidered with elaborate Celtic knotwork. Shimmery translucent wings attached to her shoulders rose up high behind her.

"Death is not the end, nor the opposite of life," Jewelia continued. "Let us honor those who walk among us in spirit. Harness this opportunity to vanquish the past, so that we may welcome in the new. I wish you all a magickal evening." Jewelia smiled and nodded as the audience clapped.

They stepped down from the podium and Delvina suddenly ran up to Varlina, swooping her up by the elbow and dragging her out on the dance floor as the mysterious waltz music began to play once more. Hannah followed, beginning to swirl her dress and toss her hair. She spotted Ashlin across the room, inviting her to join her with the curling of her finger.

Ashlin waved and moved toward Hannah on the dance floor. Their bodies began to sync with the notes of the music. As they approached each other to the beat, they moved their hands in the air, making shapes with their fingers. Their bodies flowed into a mysterious dance, each taking a turn leading and dipping the other. The music began to surround them, and it was as if glowing orbs were lifting them off the ground. They became lost in a vibrational world, carried away from the ball into a flowing river of harmonic resonance.

Hannah felt a strong wave of frisson sweeping her body as the music rose and fell, uniting with her spirit. It seemed like the dance lasted for hours, but eventually the music faded away and she and Ashlin, sweaty and happy, made their way across the theater toward a back stairwell to get some air.

"There you two are! I've been looking all over for you," Varlina said, discovering Hannah and Ashlin standing in the shadows at the top of the stairs. A fluffy Norwegian forest cat sat on the railing between them, his long fur hanging down over the wood and his inquisitive whiskers swaying in the air. "Who needs another champagne?" She motioned toward a table against a far wall.

Hannah's attention was split between Varlina and the edge of the crowd, near the table. She noticed, in particular, the tall man in the dark cloak and ominous blind mask who had tried to send her a drink earlier. She still could not make out his face, nor see his eyes, but she had a distinct feeling that the look in them was not one of joyful frivolity. He appeared to be staring at Jewelia and Morgan across the room. The visible parts of his face began to contract in a serious and ominous grimace. He was looking around but never talking to anyone. It made Hannah uneasy. *Did she know him? What was he up to? What was it about him that bothered her?* She couldn't tell. But she also couldn't shake the feeling that it wasn't good.

She leaned over to Varlina. "Who is that?"

"Hmm, I can't say as I know. A tourist, perhaps?" she replied distractedly.

"He looks out of place," Hannah said, voicing her feelings of trepidation.

"How can you tell? He's got a costume on." Varlina smirked, not understanding Hannah's concern.

"I don't know what it is, but there's something not right about him," Hannah whispered, feeling the stare of his dark eyes from behind his mask as he turned his head. She shuddered and decided to move out of his sight. Hours passed and Hannah made her rounds, visiting with the other shop keepers in town and patrons from the lounge. Eventually, she knew Wendy would appreciate help cleaning up, so she headed down the stairs toward the appetizer area.

"Can I help you with all this?" Hannah offered when she found Wendy. She began to grab discarded plates and toss them in the trash.

"That would be great. Can you go into the back room and grab my rolling cart? It will make it easier to move all of this," Wendy suggested.

"Of course." Hannah spun around to head toward the back of the theater.

She parted the thick curtains that separated the lively Masquerade Ball from the quiet and solemn back room. Her heels clicked upon the hardwood floor as she cautiously let her eyesight adjust. As she wandered in the darkness, her mind began to drift. Walking slowly, with her hands in front of her, she fumbled for the light switch. She had never been in the back area and was surprised how spacious it was. Along the walls were old sepia photos of the town. Hannah stepped closer, peering into each one, imagining what the island was like back then. She began to wonder about her ancestors. *Why had they come here anyway? What terrible force had led them to leave their homeland?*

Her heart quickened when she heard a loud thump. She began to worry that the masked man might be back there with her. She proceeded to walk quicker, then spun back around and headed toward the thick curtains. After the tunnel incident, she was becoming increasingly paranoid.

"Did you get it?" Wendy asked as Hannah returned.

"Get what?" Hannah asked, confused.

"The cart? In the back room?" Wendy looked concerned.

"Oh right, I totally forgot, sorry. I'll go grab it."

"That's okay, we can manage without. Here, grab these," she said, passing Hannah large boxes filled with the remaining appetizers.

"All set?" Delvina came gliding over.

"Yes, we've got it, thanks," Hannah confirmed, finishing up and tracking down Ashlin near the fireplace. "Hey, let's get out of here. I'm wiped," she said, acting like she was just tired.

"Sure, I'm ready to go," Ashlin obliged.

They said their goodbyes to Nutmeg and the twins, then stopped to bid good night to Jewelia and Morgan on the way out.

In year's past, she never wanted the ball to end, but this year she felt different. Maybe it was because she just couldn't shake the foreboding feeling she'd had since the prophecy. Seeing the images of Maple Hollow so long ago made her more curious about the forces her ancestors had faced. Was her whole family being stalked by this masked stranger? The unease was beginning to spread in ways she hadn't prepared for. Maybe this was why she felt worse; her intuition was confirming her body's suspicion. Maybe they really were in danger.

CHAPTER TEN

THE MASK

Tired from the ball, Hannah started to get ready for bed. As she took off the cloak she had worn, she reached into the pocket and found Wendy's menu. She had looked at it so briefly before diving into the tastings that she hadn't noticed there was more writing on the back. In neat penmanship, Wendy had written down the special properties of each of the ingredients for her. Hannah began to review them.

Cardamom offers anti-bacterial benefits. Clove is anti-microbial. Rosemary is an antiseptic. Cinnamon not only is an anti-viral but also aids one in spiritual insights, and can be used for protection and healing.

She began to wonder why Wendy had chosen these herbs and spices. Perhaps she knew about Hannah's afflictions but hadn't said anything to her?

Hannah placed the menu onto the nightstand and got cozy in her bed. As she closed her eyes, she contemplated the botanicals. Eventually she fell into a deep sleep.

***

She found herself in the great hall of Skye Manor, facing the large stone fireplace. She was alone in the room, her eyes fixed upon the dancing flames. Her mind began to listen, as if the blazing fire was whispering to her. She began to hear a message:

Remove the Mask
Embrace the Power
Face the Flames
At the Final Hour

Then she abruptly awoke. Hannah reached for her dream journal and began to scribble down the riddle she had received. As she wrote *Remove the Mask*, the image of the dark figure at the ball suddenly popped into her mind. Perhaps the riddle was calling her to unmask his identity. *Embrace the Power* sounded very similar to what Jewelia had instructed her to do in the letter she'd written to Hannah long ago, asking her to come to Maple Hollow. But what power was this riddle referring to? She pondered the lines, also wondering what *Face the Flames* might mean.

When she had vanquished Norma Nyx, the Dream Haunter, six years ago, she did so by staring into the fire and envisioning her ceasing to exist. By facing the flames, she had become one with them, her essence engaging in an ethereal dance with the fire. Later, Hannah had discovered that she actually had an ability to divine through the flames, called pyromancy by some: by observing the color of the flames, the way they flickered, the height they reached, and their rise and fall, she could in fact receive information.

But the part of the riddle that stopped her in her tracks was the phrase *the Final Hour*. That didn't sound good at all, and too similar to the possibility of demise in the prophecy. Whose final hour? Hers? Someone she cared about? What was this riddle trying to tell her?

She also thought about the fire, several years ago, that had burned a portion of Maple Moon, Morgan's metaphysical shop and her home above it. There certainly had been flames in that situation, from which Morgan's two cats, Merlin and Milu, had thankfully escaped. The cause of the fire had never been discovered, but she had always suspected foul play.

Hannah set down the dream journal and looked toward her bedside table. Next to her alarm clock was a small vase filled with bright orange chrysanthemums. She reached across the bed and extended her fingers to grasp one of the stems. She suddenly remembered her old dreams about Leaf, her magickal forest guide; Leaf's body was essentially a stem. Then she began to stare deeply into the center of the mum. She adjusted her gaze, like she had learned to do with mirrors, and began to look through it rather than at it.

After a moment, the flower almost began to swirl like a kaleidoscope, its pattern a circular mandala of precise angles repeating into infinitum. Hannah closed her eyes and could see clearly, in her third eye, a spinning circle. As she breathed, it began to spin faster and faster. She thought about the Narcissus flower that had poisoned Wendy's friend Jezebelle when she came to visit. Consumed by relentless vanity and pride in her physical appearance, Jezebelle had plotted to steal the fabled flower that would secure eternal beauty; in doing so, she'd awoken the Illusionix, a trickster entity that made reflections seem real and caused people to lose their sense of agency and self. Jezebelle had poisoned herself in this endeavor, and only through Hannah's ability to destroy the Illusionix was Jezebelle freed, and able to recognize that her body was merely a mask her spirit was wearing.

Hannah had recognized that she too was always learning, after all these years, how to remove her metaphorical mask. The one that had blocked her self-esteem since childhood. The one that was her worst inner critic. As the image of the mum continued to spin in her mind, it began to dissolve into the ether, becoming one with its surroundings. As Hannah reflected upon Jezebelle's transformation, she had a flash of realization.

"The mask is the ego!" she said out loud. The mask, she realized, is what we all must shed to embrace our power.

But still, she couldn't shake the foreboding words *the Final Hour*. Did that mean the final hour of life? If so, whose? She hoped it wasn't her own.

CHAPTER ELEVEN

THE AURORA

Hannah had trouble falling back asleep and decided to leave her bedroom for a bit. She walked down the long corridor toward the bathroom. The hallway was lit on each side by small lanterns, the flickering flames dancing within them. As she passed the mirrors along the walls, she saw something unexpected. It wasn't just stars, but a swirling brightness of dancing colors. Hannah gazed into the mirrors, not sure whether she should look at the beauty displayed there or beyond. As she watched the ebb and flow of the colors dance, she realized it was actually a reflection of the sky. Each mirror caught a different part of the sky, but together they reflected back the vast expanse of it.

She turned slowly toward the mullioned picture window midway down the hall and looked out across the manor grounds. Gazing at the sky above the sea, Hannah saw the most magnificent sight she'd ever seen. Her heart quickened with excitement. She grabbed a silver lantern from the end of the hallway and stepped lightly but quickly down the stairs, holding it above her waist with her left hand and steadying herself on the banister with her right.

She made it to the bottom, crossed the foyer, and passed through the darkness of the hallway at the back of the house, which led to the back door. Grabbing a cloak from a hook, she stepped outside. The glow enveloped her. Hannah's face lit up with the reflection of the vibrant aurora borealis in the sky.

As she looked up, her heart was flooded with an emotion she had never felt before. Tears filled her eyes as she realized that the sky, filled with brilliant tones of green, purple, and pink, was dancing. It was moving faster than anything she had ever seen. Towers of light surrounded her, painting the vast darkness. Small sections raced across the horizon like flames of fire, dancing and flickering faster. The whole sky was moving like an underwater dance.

She walked slowly down the cypress-lined path, toward the sea. As she drew closer to the water, she saw there was yet another reflection of the sky in the water. Sometimes the sea could be tumultuous, waves crashing onto the shore, but now the sea was still, like glass. The sky and the sea became one canvas, each a mirror image of the other.

As Hannah stood staring at the amazing scene, she began to ponder the significance. *What was causing the sky to glow? Why now? Could everyone see these lights, or did they just present themselves at certain times for certain people?*

She watched the parade of blues, purples, and greens, sometimes stretching across, sometimes swirling up into tall towers of light. Amongst the dancing curtains of color were twinkling stars. And there was one constellation of intense activity, where everything around it appeared to be called in...a cluster of stars. Beams of light were shooting toward the center, one after the other, chasing into the dark abyss. Each taking their turn, jumping in unafraid.

She stood, watching the Northern Lights in awe as the dance continued, the flames flickering in her lantern and casting a light amongst the shadows on the ground. There were no clouds and no fog. In their place was a crystal-clear sense of clarity and transmission. It was as if she were watching a language of light communicating a message through movement.

She didn't have the words nor the actions to express how it made her spirit soar. She felt as if the sky was full of spirits. And that they were inviting her to join them. The union and celebration of light filled her soul. Her body could scarcely contain the beauty.

Hannah walked back to her bedroom, filled with wonder. Over the years, she had faithfully recorded her dreams, and ever since moving to Maple Hollow, this had been key to keeping away the Dream Haunters. But she had also acquired a new technique. Before going to sleep, she would ask her dreams for answers. Since receiving the prophecy with Ashlin, many questions weighed on her mind. Ones that she could not answer in the conscious realm. She knew that the wisdom she sought was hiding within the subconscious. And she was going to draw it out.

Back in her room, she placed the small stones she found in the tunnel under her pillow, before slipping under the covers and pulling the sheets up to her chin. The third riddle still echoed in her mind. Before long, she fell into a deep sleep.

***

She found herself at a large log cabin; it seemed as if a retreat was happening there. She stepped out onto an expansive deck that overlooked a mountain vista of snow-covered peaks and lush evergreen trees. There were many people socially milling about.

A woman who had been sitting on the patio stood up and greeted her. To Hannah's surprise, the woman said, "We have been waiting for you." There was a gentle air about her that put Hannah at ease, although she did wonder who "we" was referring to.

The scene quickly shifted and suddenly she found herself flying through the air, surrounded by puffy white clouds. There were three women flying on either side of her and one behind. She was effortlessly moving forward, rapidly through the air, her arms resting casually at her sides. A smile crossed Hannah's lips as she felt a surge of confidence and solace.

"Release and be at peace," she heard in her mind as they crossed the vast skyscape together.

CHAPTER TWELVE

THE STARS

OCTOBER 27, 2013

Hannah woke up. It was still dark and Midnight was curled in a ball underneath her left arm, purring by her heart. When she rustled, he leapt up from his comfortable place of repose like he had been flung into the air by a springboard. She grabbed for her journal. She had been flying through the air in her dream, just like Midnight was, but there were others with her, other women. In fact, there were seven women. Three on each side and one who she felt guiding her from behind. They had been waiting for her. It reminded her of the dream she'd had once about an owl who told her she'd been watched for seven years. Seven?! There was that number again. Could these have been the Seven Sisters of Skye?

As she quickly wrote the flying dream in her journal, Hannah thought back to the Masquerade Ball and the ominous masked man. That had been followed by seeing the aurora, which was miraculously beautiful and had evoked in her a sensation similar to the flying feeling in her dream. The dancing Northern Lights had appeared to emanate from a constellation...but which one?

Hannah ran downstairs, ducking through the demure door tucked under the staircase and emerging into the manor's magnificent library. She loved this room, where bookshelves, filled with candles, photos, and trinkets, arched up to a wondrous ceiling. There was a large telescope in one corner that she'd never paid much attention to. She immediately went for the eyepiece, angled it toward a window, and started to scan the pre-dawn skies. When she saw the constellations, her pulse began to quicken. Midnight, who had scurried in behind her, attempted to distract her, but she kept her focus on the sky.

Then Hannah started searching the floor-to-ceiling shelves for a book on astronomy. When she finally found one, she sat down in a soft upholstered chair next to a Tiffany floor lamp and flipped through the pages. Midnight promptly jumped on her lap. She could have simply communed with the book, but this time she wanted to search by the images. The memory of what she had seen through the telescope was fading.

In the center of the book was a large page, made of thicker paper, that unfolded to reveal color illustrations. It showed all of the constellations of the night sky. Hannah scanned with her fingers until she found it, then correlated the key of the celestial map to the description on the following page:

The Pleiades, often called the Seven Sisters, is actually a cluster of stars. It is comprised of more than 1,000 stars. Located in the constellation of Taurus, it is estimated to be over 400 light years from Earth.

Hannah continued to read about the ancient mythology behind the constellation and the various legends of the Seven Sisters. The story was that they were created from a blending of air and water elements: a god of the sky named Atlas and a nymph of the ocean. The book explained that there was an easy way to find the Pleiades in the sky, first by locating another cluster of "sisters," a group of three inside Orion. This cluster only emerged into visibility in the dark portion of the year. The book explained that another star, Aldebaran, followed the Seven Sisters and was known as a mysterious portal of illumination, transformation, and revelations.

Hannah had always felt drawn to the Pleiades, but she had never been sure why. Certainly, there were millions of fascinating stars in the sky, more than she could ever imagine, and galaxies beyond that. But there was something that drew her, and now that she had received the prophecy from the sisters, flown through the sky with them, and witnessed the aurora, she knew it was no coincidence.

CHAPTER THIRTEEN

THE FLARES

Her stomach grumbling, Hannah hurried down to the kitchen. Wendy had brought tasters from the ball back to the manor and spread them out for breakfast. There was no shortage of delectable treats to start her day with.

"Good morning, Wendy," Hannah said as she sat down and reached for a donut hole.

"It certainly is! The sun is shining brightly today, isn't it?"

"The sky was so clear last night. I saw the Northern Lights!" Hannah exclaimed, excited to tell someone.

"Oh, you did?" Jewelia asked, sounding equally excited as she entered the kitchen and surveyed the bounty.

"Hey, Jewelia, I meant to ask you, how exactly does that telescope in the library work? I decided to check it out this morning and it's amazing!"

"Ah, you'll appreciate this." Jewelia helped herself to some coffee. "I'm not surprised that you were drawn to it. That is a reflecting telescope. It uses mirrors!"

"You're kidding? But of course, it does," Hannah exclaimed at the synchronicity.

"There are other kinds, but ours is the type that uses two mirrors—one that gathers the light and one that directs the light inward."

"So, it's not just magnification, it's actually reflection?"

"Correct," Jewelia responded, nodding. "It brings us much closer to the grandness of the universe. The infinite web we are all part of. Interconnected."

Hannah understood Jewelia's insight. "In a way, it does make us reflect about the unseen realms."

"That it does," Jewelia agreed.

They all sat quietly, sipping their warm morning drinks and perusing the flavorful creations.

Afterward, Hannah rode her bike into town to see Ashlin at the Maple Hollow Library. She wanted to discuss the events of the Masquerade Ball, and also her dreams. As she peddled down the quaint seaside streets, she savored the salty air, the crisp breeze, and the autumn landscape. It truly was beautiful and lifted her spirits. She rounded the tree-lined path to the charming Victorian building. Leaving her bike near the archway entry, she burst in and immediately discovered Ashlin arranging a large stack of books.

"I had this dream last night that I was flying through the sky with seven women!" Hannah declared.

"Good morning! Seven women?" Ashlin said, startled at her arrival.

"It was so amazing. They said they were waiting for me."

"Waiting for what? Do you think it was the seven sisters in the prophecy?"

"I'm beginning to think so! Jewelia told me she's heard of the Seven Sisters of Skye. They were the ones who founded Maple Hollow." Hannah started to help

Ashlin with the books, but as she bent over, her phone started beeping in her pocket.

"Who's that?" Ashlin asked.

"Not who, but what," Hannah explained. "It's a notification. I downloaded this app on my phone that notifies me whenever there is significant moon or sun activity."

"Wow, that's so cool," Ashlin said. "Show me!"

"I've been extensively researching astronomical and celestial occurrences recently. Now that I can commune with books, the way you do, it makes research significantly faster."

"It sure does," Ashlin said, taking Hannah's phone into her hands and peering at the glass.

"For some reason, I've always felt drawn to the night sky, outer space, and what's beyond the earthly realm. When I look up at the sky of stars, I feel connected in a way I can't explain. It's always been a source of endless fascination for me. And guess what—I saw the aurora borealis last night!"

"I did too! Wasn't it amazing?" Ashlin exclaimed.

"Yes, it was breathtaking. I also saw it reflected in the sea. The lights were magnificent."

"I know what you mean. Astronomy has always captivated me," Ashlin mused as she continued to sort the books. "As a society, we think we know what's out there, but I'm sure there is so much more than we currently understand."

"I've been compiling facts about astronomy and space science, even the physics of the sun. Did you know that the sun is actually a star, just a very close one?" Hannah said.

"Yes, that's right," Ashlin confirmed.

"The sun generates light, but the moon, like a mirror, simply reflects it."

"A reflection in the darkness."

"Beyond our sun, there are billions of stars in just our small galaxy, bigger and brighter," Hannah continued. "In fact, the sun is said to be an over-four-billion-year-old star. Constantly evolving and transforming, it sometimes has storms of its own. Essentially, there are huge explosions that happen within the sun's atmosphere that send electromagnetic radiation hurtling toward Earth. Scientists call them solar flares—one of the phenomena of the astronomical realm."

"So how often do these flares happen?" Ashlin asked.

"They're more common during peak periods of solar activity. There have been so many solar flares happening lately, my phone has been buzzing out of control. And they're increasing with rapid intensity."

"How do you know how intense they are?"

"Astronomers have classified certain types of solar flares on a letter scale, kind of like earthquakes: X being the most powerful. Each letter marks a ten-time increase from the last."

"Are they intense right now?" Ashlin asked.

"Yes, they started Thursday night, around the time we met at the manor for the ritual. I had my phone off, but once I turned it back on, I got four notifications. And then apparently there were four more on Friday night while I was in the tunnel. Last night, during the ball, there were two more, and another one after that. And guess what I dreamed about last night?" Hannah paused dramatically.

"What?"

"The third riddle!" Hannah quickly recited the verse.

"Um, the *Final Hour*? We don't need another message about impending doom," Ashlin grimaced. She peered at the phone as Hannah scrolled. "Wow, they really are going crazy right now."

"There have been thirteen X-class flares this year alone! They're supposed to peak again tomorrow night, leading up to a really big one on Tuesday," Hannah said. "The bigger the flare, the larger the impact. Did you know they can cause worldwide blackouts?"

"Really?" Ashlin lifted a large pile of books and, giving a friendly nod to a patron who had just entered, moved toward one of the stacks to shelve them.

Hannah followed her. "Apparently, the massive energy that surges from our sun can affect us at a cellular level. We can feel energized, or hazy, like we're walking in a dense fog. It can also cause sleep disturbances apparently. I wonder if that's my problem."

"That makes so much sense. I haven't been sleeping well this week myself."

"Of course, there's a beautiful side effect of the aurora, so maybe it's worth it," Hannah said. "When you think about how a thunderstorm works—there are storms both on Earth *and* in space. There is, after all, weather there too. And just like the powerful force of lightning, solar flares are transformational catalysts."

"Storms do bring change, metaphorically," Ashlin agreed.

"They are essentially solar storms, which create huge clouds of charged particles. They're drawn in by the magnetism of the earth's poles. And when the particles collide with the atmosphere of earth, they heat up, which makes them glow. This is what produces the amazing phenomenon of the aurora borealis. The aurora itself is technically a deflection that happens where the magnetic fields are weak. So, we in fact see a reflection of a deflection."

"That's wild! There are so many fascinating legends about the aurora borealis," Ashlin said. "Some cultures believe the lights are messages from departed souls, sending guidance to spirits that still remain on the earthly plane. Others believe the celestial dance of lights tells a story—sometimes an ominous warning, sometimes a magickal message of hope and good fortune. There are even those who once believed that the Earth was hollow and that there was a sun inside the planet, which the aurora was a reflection of."

"An inner sun? Interesting. What did the Celtic people believe?" Hannah asked.

"In Celtic legend, the goddess Arianrhod lives in an Otherworld revolving castle in the sky. The curtains of lights are claimed to be the lights of her castle," Ashlin said.

"Arianrhod!" Hannah was surprised. "I read about her in a book on owls. It said she's a messenger of the subconscious. I've often wondered if she was the owl who appeared at our dinner with Jezebelle."

"It's possible! In ancient mythologies, the lights are believed to be the spirits of the departed, engaged in a dance that provides messages and guidance to the living."

"I like that. It did look like a dance in the sky, and I felt like there was a deeper message within it for me, from the spirits," Hannah said.

She scanned the app further, continuing to study the historical activity. "So, get this," she said, trailing Ashlin into the next aisle of books. "Apparently the largest solar flare ever recorded happened at Halloween, just four years before I discovered Maple Hollow. It was so large, it was off the charts."

"I wonder what *that* means!" Ashlin stopped in her tracks and raised a curious eyebrow.

CHAPTER FOURTEEN

THE COMPASS CLOCK

Hannah and Ashlin left the library and stopped at a nearby bistro that overlooked the sea for lunch. They sipped cups of steamy soup and continued their chat about the intriguing mythology of the skies and solar system. Eventually, they parted ways and Hannah headed back to the manor. Once she made it onto the grounds, she went straight to Old Man Adams' cabin. She felt in her bones that in order to understand the prophecy, she needed more information about her own family line than she'd been able to discover over the years. Maple leaves gently cascaded down along her path, lightly crunching under her feet as the crisp air of fall filled her lungs.

She lifted her hand and knocked three times on the wooden door.

"Well, hello, little lady," Old Man Adams announced, opening the door and immediately stepping back to let Hannah in.

"Hello," she said. "Hope I'm not intruding."

"Not at all! Please come in. Can I get you some tea?"

"Sure, that'd be great."

Adams disappeared into the kitchen, pots and pans clamoring for a bit, and then returned carrying two small cups of water and a tiny tin of tea bags, shuffling his slippers across the wood floor toward two cozy armchairs and a small side table facing the fireplace.

"What brings you today?" he asked as he set down the mugs and leaned back into his chair.

"I've been thinking lately about my parents," Hannah started in. "More than usual. I know we've talked about it before, but I still feel like I don't have the whole story about why they never told me about Maple Hollow before they died."

"Have you talked to Jewelia about this?"

"Actually, I thought talking to you again might be better. Since she and my father are siblings and all, I feel like there is a level of complication to her answers."

"Well, that makes sense," Adams said, taking a deep breath indicative of his burden of bearing the information.

"So...what can you tell me?"

"What do you want to know?"

"I want to know why my father left the manor. This is such an amazing, beautiful place. I really don't understand why anyone would leave. I know you said that he just wanted to go his own way. And I get that it's natural to want to leave home. But is that all there was to it? Or were there other factors involved? In other words, even once he left and married my mother...why did he never come back?"

Old Man Adams shifted in his chair. The expression on his face and his avoidance of eye contact indicated to Hannah that he was searching for the right words, and perhaps felt a little put on the spot.

"Okay, you are very intuitive, little lady. It's only natural for you to question, I suppose. We just don't talk about it—best to leave those types of things in the past, if you know what I mean."

"No, I don't know. Tell me, why did he leave?"

"It's possible, and I'm really just speculating here, that he was trying to avoid the curse."

Hannah sat up straight in her chair. "Curse? What curse?"

"Well, it's all ancient history, but I suppose there could be some truth to it. Hard to tell."

"What do you mean? What curse? On who?"

"There is a legend that your family fled their homeland because they were cursed. I don't know all the details, but someone supposedly cursed a group of women, condemning them each to suffer a tragic demise that would be passed down through their descendants. It has supposedly played out over time. We'll never know if it was just a coincidence. Your father, Will, didn't want this fate to befall him or his family. But perhaps he could not escape it."

"How do you know about this curse?"

"I've been here so long, I forget where I heard of it. When your grandparents passed, I received a letter stating that I was named in the estate. I came here to the manor, and found out they had left it, and your Aunt Jewelia, in my care. I've been living here ever since. They also left me something else. I still have it, somewhere." Adams got up and scurried over to one of his bookshelves. "Here you are, little lady. It's probably time that you have this," he said, passing a compass into Hannah's slender outstretched palm.

"It's beautiful," Hannah said as she ran her fingers over the engraving of a key on the front. At first, she simply recognized it from the family crest she had seen on the gated entrance to the manor: a key in a circle, crossed over with a treble clef. But then suddenly, she remembered a dream she'd had when she first came to the island. It was storming, and she was standing near a lighthouse, soaked with rain. She had reached into her pocket and pulled out an antique compass. The arms had spun erratically at first, gaining their bearings, but then their motion had slowed like a pendulum. It was then that the skies parted, the rain had ceased, and the stars began to twinkle, illuminating the sky.

"It used to work, pretty good actually, but now I think it's finally broken. Ironically, it would always start spinning when you or your aunt were in danger," Adams shared, interrupting her dream memory.

Hannah pressed the small knob on the top of the compass, popping it open. Inside, she was surprised to find that it wasn't just a compass, but also a watch, an elegant timepiece with ornamental hands that were pointing to midnight.

Adams pointed. "That there is a gyrocompass."

"What's that?"

"It uses the Earth's rotation for direction rather than magnetic fields. And it's also a clock. They work together, I guess. One setting the target and the other setting the tempo."

"How interesting," Hannah said, liking the musical analogy. "Does the clock still work?"

"I'm not sure. But even so, it's still right twice a day," Adams said, winking.

As Old Man Adams continued to recount his coming to the manor, Hannah's fingers explored the compass. She turned it to and fro, catching the light. As she ran her nails around the bezel, she realized there was a notch above the number 12. She dug her nail in further as it began to give way. Adams' eyes widened as he watched.

"There's something here," Hannah said, prying it open.

Behind the face of the clock was a small piece of aged paper. Hannah gently removed it and unfolded it slowly.

Old Man Adams leaned in. "Well, what have you got there?" he asked in genuine surprise.

"It looks like a note," Hannah said. "A note from my grandfather?" She flattened it out on the table and brought an oil lamp closer for a better view.

"It's just a drawing," Adams said, grimacing in confusion and disappointment.

"Spirals!" Hannah blurted, remembering the sand on the mirror during the prophecy. "These are spirals."

"But what does it mean?"

"I don't know, but I'm going to find out. Who else knows about this curse?"

"Ashlin might, since she knows the island's history. To be honest, I'm not sure if I've ever discussed it with Jewelia. She was young and confused when I moved here to take care of her and Will, and as the years raced on, it seemed better to let it go. I wanted a fresh life for her, without the heavy weight of the past."

"So did my father know about the curse?"

"Since he was older, I did tell him," Adams said regretfully, scratching his chin with his hand. "I suspect that's why he left the island."

Hannah sat back in her chair in shock and disbelief at the circumstances and story that had been revealed. She felt validated in her suspicion that she never knew the full story, but frustrated that so much had been kept from her. Now she had to question Jewelia. The silence had gone on long enough.

Chapter Fifteen

THE CURSE

Hannah ran toward the manor. She loved her aunt, but she needed to make sense of this revelation. Jewelia had taught her so much about the island, and about how to access and grow in her own magick, but somehow, she had never gotten around to this topic.

Busting through the back door and into the kitchen, Hannah found the room cold and quiet. No fire in the fireplace. No smells of warm bread cooking in the oven. No swirls of steam from boiling pots on the stove. She turned around and went straight up the stairs to Jewelia's bedroom.

"That's why he left!" were the first words she blurted out, not wasting any time.

Jewelia looked up, alarm and surprise on her face. "I'm sorry, what?" she said anxiously, unaware of what could warrant this unannounced intrusion.

"My father...I know why he left Maple Hollow. Old Man Adams told me about the curse on our family. Did you keep this from me all this time?"

The stunned look on Jewelia's face changed to one of remorse, sadness, and defeat as she realized what Hannah was upset about.

"My love, that is ancient history," she finally said. "Someday you might understand. I'm sorry I didn't tell you. It wasn't that I was trying to purposely keep it from you. I guess I was rather keeping it from myself."

"So, our family has had a curse upon it this whole time." Hannah took a deep breath to calm herself. She had allowed her blood to rise in her veins, racing to her mind and fogging her thoughts. She knew in her soul that her aunt had not betrayed her, but she was especially sensitive during Mercury retrograde and this news just added to her agitation about the prophecy. She knew Jewelia had her own reasons for her silence, but the only way to understand this was to open her heart, not close it.

She took a deep breath. "Old Man Adams gave me Grandpa's compass," she said, producing it from her pocket.

"Compass?" A new look of surprise crossed Jewelia's face as she sensed the shift in Hannah's demeanor. "Let me see!" She took it and admired it. "I've heard tales of this. It's unique—not only because it tells direction *and* time, but because it operates outside of the 3D realm. It has its own catalytic force that controls it..." She trailed off, her eyes staring into the beyond.

"I found this inside it." Hannah produced the worn note from her pocket. "Do you know what this drawing means?"

Jewelia looked at the note, her face blank. "I'm afraid I don't," she sighed.

"It must have something to do with the curse. The prophecy Ashlin and I received in the ritual was surrounded by spirals in the sand on the mirror. They looked very similar to this. In fact, I think there were seven! We know we're being sent a message from our ancestors, the Seven Sisters of Skye. And now, knowing all this, I think that prophecy is related to the curse. Adams said the curse had something to do with each woman suffering a tragic demise. That could possibly explain my parents, and yours, too!"

"Sometimes it's just our time," Jewelia offered, still seeming to hold discussion of the curse at arm's length.

Hannah had heard this phrase in the past when others had tried to console her and explain why her parents had died in an accident. But the word "time" struck Hannah in a way it hadn't before. There were so many metaphysical theories about why we are here on Earth and what determines when we go. When people died, was their work completed? Or were they being called somewhere else to do more work? Was everyone reincarnated, or was there a point in existence where the cycle ended and people ascended to serve as guides in the Otherworld?

As Hannah stared at the still hands of the compass clock, she didn't mention to Jewelia that she hadn't been feeling well lately. She understood in that moment why people sometimes choose silence. Her body was beginning to speak to her mind, and she was getting the distinct feeling that it was going to be her duty to discover not only what the curse was, but *who* had cursed her family. The ancestral trauma had gone on for too long, and it was up to her to put an end to the generational suffering.

Chapter Sixteen

THE PARADOXUM

Hannah trotted down the stairs, pulling out her phone to dial Ashlin before she headed to her shift at the Whispering Whiskers. "I have so much to tell you," she exclaimed when her friend answered.

"I was just thinking about you!" Ashlin whispered, to not disturb the patrons of the library. "I've found information that helps explain your dis-ease."

"I can't wait to hear," Hannah said. "Let's meet up later at the lounge? I'll be off around nine."

"Of course. Everything okay?" Ashlin asked, a note of trepidation entering her voice.

"I'm not sure. But I'll explain when I see you."

Hannah stepped out the front door of the manor, letting the autumn sun warm her face. It was beginning to sink into the horizon, splashing broad streaks of orange and pink across the sky. The large maple trees were blackening against the painted backdrop, rising in stark contrast to the golden glow.

Crisp, cool air rose into her nostrils as she quickened her pace toward town. She was anxious to talk to Ashlin. She was beginning to think there were more than medical reasons for her ailment, whatever it was.

These distracting thoughts continued all through her shift. Hannah barely paid attention to what she was playing, really just going through the motions. She scarcely even noticed the patrons as they entered and exited the lounge. She began to emerge from her fog of distress when she realized what time it was and heard Ashlin's familiar voice behind her.

"Are you all done?" her friend asked, her arms outstretched toward Hannah for a hug.

"You snuck in! I didn't even see you," Hannah said. "Yes, all done, let's go grab a table."

They walked over to a private table that had a small pumpkin candle placed in the middle, the flickering flame dancing upon the wick. Behind them, a large tabby cat jumped up onto a small shelf, ready to eavesdrop on their conversation.

"And what will it be tonight?" the waitress asked.

"I'll have a chai," Hannah said, having had enough to drink the night before. She sat back in her chair and watched the cats chase each other in circles to ease her mind.

"The tea of the day for me, please," Ashlin said, closing the menu.

"On the way." The waitress disappeared through the maze of tables toward the bar, dancing between resident cats who were starting their nightly nocturnal chase routines.

"They're always wound up at this time of night," Ashlin laughed, watching them.

"Before we get into talking about my dis-ease," Hannah said with a grimace, "what else can you tell me about our ancestors coming to the island?"

"Well, as you know, they fled their homeland and created Maple Hollow as a sanctuary where each of the families could protect its magick," Ashlin replied. She paused and took a sip of her water. "It was all initiated by a group of women who needed to escape—apparently called the Seven Sisters of Skye. Others in their land were condemning them for their powers. It was a witch hunt of the worst kind."

"Did those people do something to them?"

"Yes. I believe it was related to the family line. A curse that each generation would experience a tragic death or something like that."

"That's exactly what Old Man Adams just told me! Why didn't you ever tell me about this curse?" Hannah said, feeling slightly hurt and betrayed.

"I guess you never asked. Nobody is really thinking about that anymore."

"But you know I've always been trying to figure out what happened to my parents, and why my father had such a strange relationship to Maple Hollow. Information about this is what I've been searching for."

"I'm sorry," Ashlin said softly. "But how did Old Man Adams know about the curse?"

"He couldn't remember. But he did give me this," Hannah passed the compass across the table to Ashlin.

"That's beautiful," Ashlin said, admiring it.

"And inside, I found this. Anything look familiar?" Hannah pushed the note across the table.

Ashlin gazed at the note, then dramatically looked up at Hannah. "You've got to be kidding," she said. "These circular lines look exactly like the sand on the mirror!"

"Right?" Hannah said, happy at the validation. "But what does it mean?" She felt exasperated.

They sat in silence as each of them mulled over the meaning of the prophecy and the symbols on the parchment.

"Well, we have less than four days to *Gather the Keys of our Legacy Power* before the seven days are up," Ashlin said finally. "I hope you receive more of the riddles soon!"

"Me too." Hannah sighed. "In the meantime, what did you find out about my dis-ease?"

"Right! I've discovered a condition that could explain what you're experiencing. Here, I'll write it down for you so you can check it out." Ashlin grabbed the napkin under her water glass and a pen from her pocket. She started to scribble down a phrase, then passed it to Hannah: *Autonemesis Paradoxum.*

"I've never heard of this," Hannah said, furrowing her brow.

"That's to be expected," Ashlin said carefully. "It's an attack caused by an imbalance in the etheric body, a dis-ease. An inner conflict, for example, that manifests itself as an affliction on the physical plane, becoming a disease of the body."

"The etheric body, what's that?" Hannah asked, confused.

"Think of it as our spiritual or energetic body that exists just outside our physical one," Ashlin explained.

"So, it's not just a normal sickness," Hannah said, her concern growing. "Is this related to the curse? Is there a cure?"

"I think I may know someone who can help. She's not really a doctor, more of a diviner...well, she's really a blacksmith," Ashlin said bluntly.

"A blacksmith? How is she going to help me?" Hannah asked, confused.

"You'd be surprised. I think that's just her cover." Ashlin winked.

"Oh, okay," Hannah said, giving her a knowing look. Maybe this blacksmith *could* help her. "You'll have to give me her information. I need all the help I can get."

"Her name is Seren Sirona. I'll send it to you right now." Ashlin picked up her phone and typed in the information.

"Sent!" she said, setting her phone back down.

"I'll go see her tomorrow," Hannah said. "Thank you so much."

"Of course, whatever I can do." Ashlin gave her a reassuring look. "Oh, and bring something metal with you—she's a blacksmith, after all! Something that's important to you would probably work best."

Hannah's curiosity was piqued. After they parted ways, instead of walking back to the manor, she side-tracked and decided to wander to the street where the blacksmith shop was. She gazed up at the small signs that hung over each entrance, advertising the tiny shops inside the brick buildings. Even though it was dark, she eventually found the weathered sign for the blacksmith shop. It hung from a metal rack that squeaked as it swung in the night sea breeze.

She stood in the dark of the street, the moon beaming down upon her, her eyes fixed upon the sign, hope in her heart. Tomorrow she would return to town and go straight to this shop. Whatever it was that Ashlin knew about her, Hannah felt intrinsically that the blacksmith could help. Ashlin would not have suggested it otherwise. She had no qualms finding answers in obscure places. Even though she didn't know where this would lead, she was ready and willing to follow the path to the answers she so desperately needed to find.

***

That night, Hannah drifted off to sleep with optimism and pessimism jockeying for position. In her dream, she approached the entrance to the great hall of the manor and saw a pulsing glow emanating from inside. It was a crystal ball, and inside it was a small galaxy filled with pulsating blue stars like the Pleiades. She was drawn toward its twinkling glow, as if a heartbeat was pulling her in.

The vibration of the little galaxy began to quicken as she reached out her fingers. She stood still, placing her hands on the crystal ball and gazing into it, her eyes widening. She began to hear quiet whispers in her mind. It was as if the globe was transferring cosmic wisdom into her consciousness.

Then Hannah found herself standing in front of the manor. The tall windows glowed in the night, towering high above her. She could see inside to the luxurious interior of each room.

She began to rise off the ground, effortlessly gliding toward the sky. As her body elevated, a thought arose within her that there must be a spectacular view from the top. Unexpectedly, her body shot high into the air.

She could clearly see, beyond the spires of the manor, places on the roof where she could easily land, and from which she would be able to see far and wide.

She looked off into the distance, to the tumbling waves of the ocean. The sky was filled with thousands of glowing stars, illuminating the dark corners of her mind. She felt sure she could rise above, had already risen above, whatever she might encounter. Even though she could not fully see the horizon, or what lay beyond it, Hannah knew that she had the ability to elevate herself, to not stay attached to the lower levels of vibration. And she no longer needed the remote she'd had in her previous dream to control her flight.

When she woke, the image of the glowing manor windows echoed in her mind as she crossed the threshold into the waking world.

CHAPTER SEVENTEEN

THE FORGE

OCTOBER 28, 2013

Hannah walked along the quaint main street of Maple Hollow. The trees blazed in their bright orange, red, and yellow hues, their leaves gently cascading toward the ground, each in their own orchestrated timeline. Once she got to the small side street where the blacksmith's shop was, she turned right. Then she stopped short, distracted by her phone buzzing. It was the celestial app, notifying her of another solar flare. There were four more forecast within the next twenty-four hours. Major solar storms were afoot.

She put her phone back in her pocket, and when she did, her fingers traced several heavy keys she had procured from the walls of the manor. Ashlin had said to bring something metal that was important, and one thing Hannah had learned during her time on the island was that she herself was the key to vanquishing any obstacles she faced. On top of that, the prophecy also talked about finding the keys to her power.

As she walked past a large stack of chopped wood, she saw the blacksmith shop from the night before.

The door was slightly ajar, so she didn't need to grasp the handle firmly. As she placed one foot over the threshold, the wood floor creaked under her weight. A small, unusual-looking animal scampered across the room, surprised by her arrival. She could hear the crackling sounds of a fire, hammering, scraping, and a continual clanking. The strong smell of coal, earth, and fire blended together, filling the air. A hint of burnt honey and wood lingered.

"Well, hello there," said a woman's kind voice, out of a low cloud of smoke.

"Hello," Hannah said automatically, not yet seeing the source of the greeting.

Then, from behind a large chimney in the middle of the room, a woman stepped out. She was dressed in a dark gray top and black pants, and over her chest was a large, heavy apron that hung around her neck and stretched to the floor. Peeking out from underneath were black, steel-toed boots.

The room was like a large workshop, filled with hammers, anvils, tongs, and tools of all sizes. The lighting was low, except for sconces with dancing flames perched upon brick columns. Hanging along the walls were long wooden tools, each with a different end point: some hooks, some baskets, some trays—each with their own purpose. Strewn on the ground were bowls of various sizes. There were small wooden tables against the walls, underneath which were large wooden barrels with open tops. The ceiling glowed with exposed beams. Heavy chains hung above the uneven floor, with worn cement blocks mortared together.

"How can I help you today?" the woman asked, holding her blackened hand out to shake Hannah's. "I'm Seren."

"Nice to meet you. I'm Hannah Skye," Hannah replied, shaking her hand and then subtly wiping the grime off on her pant leg. "Ashlin Aldona sent me."

"Ah, Ashlin, yes, our families go way back," Seren said, running her fingers through her hair. It was thick, straight, black, and stuck out at all angles.

Hannah paused for a moment, wondering exactly what Seren knew about Ashlin that she did not, but quickly remembered why she was there. Then something caught her eye.

"Sorry, is that a cat?" she asked with some confusion. The small animal was rubbing against Seren's leg. It was the size of a cat, but it had much larger eyes and much less hair than usual. Its fur, or what there was of it, was wiry and sparse, and she could see its exposed toes, more than on a usual cat. It had enchanting eyes that stared into Hannah's soul, the light from the fire reflecting in them.

"This is Liraen," Seren said conversationally. "She's what they call a wolf cat—a little wolf."

"A wolf cat?" Hannah exclaimed. "I've never heard of such a thing!"

"She's harmless, I assure you. Just unique." Seren picked her up and patted her on the back. "Tell me what can I do for you, Hannah?" she asked again.

"I'm looking for some help," Hannah said. Not sure exactly what to say about what she needed, she produced the handful of silver keys from her pocket.

"Keys? I can make you copies of those." Seren held out her hand for them. "These hands and my forge can make anything!"

"I'm actually not looking to make copies, really," Hannah began hesitantly. After a pause, she added, "I haven't been feeling well lately." She wasn't sure how to ask for what she wanted. She wasn't even sure it made sense. Would Seren understand what she was trying to imply?

"Ah. You're looking for something a bit more on the metaphysical side," Seren mused, setting Liraen down.

"Yes, I..." Hannah felt her left eye began to twitch.

"I see," Seren said, her expression turning to one of compassion and intrigue. "I don't just make swords and knives here, of course." A wry smile crossed her face. "I make potions as well, but more on the metallurgical side than others might."

Hannah suddenly felt more at ease. "Yes, that's exactly what I'm looking for. I've discovered I have an ailment. I believe these keys can help me get better."

"Won't you come to my kitchen?" Seren walked toward the back of the room, and Hannah and Liraen following curiously.

Once they crossed the threshold, they were in a large room that was a dramatic contrast to the blacksmith forge. It was magickal, colorful, and inviting.

"This is where I do my metaphysical work," Seren explained. "It's not all forging blades and tools. Blending metals is like bending time. I have been gifted with the ability to not only transform matter, but heal with it as well. This is why Ashlin sent you. Her family has worked with mine for centuries. Our old ways are interwoven like a rich tapestry, a river running through a deep canyon."

"This room is beautiful. I love how it feels in here."

"I call it my kitchen because I make things here we can consume as humans, but it is also a healing sanctuary," Seren said. "Please make yourself comfortable. Everything in this room has extraordinary healing powers."

Hannah watched Liraen jump onto a regal purple chaise in the corner. It was definitely not something she would expect to find in the back of a blacksmith shop. The room was filled with colorful scarves, wall hangings, and beautiful rugs across the floor.

"Sounds lovely, thanks. But how can furniture be healing, if you don't mind me asking?" she inquired, a touch of doubt in her voice.

"The threads of this chaise are woven with the most rare and valuable amethysts from all over the globe. They were selected by my predecessors for their unique healing ability. When you recline your body, the electromagnetic waves from the crystals dance with the energetic field of your body, resetting its rhythm into one that is more harmonic and aligned."

"Crystals..." Hannah said as she passed her hand slowly over the fabric. "That's genius."

"Please, make yourself comfortable." Seren placed small pillows around Hannah on the chaise, patting them and encouraging her to recline.

"Thanks," Hannah said as she leaned back and took in the sights and smells of the room.

"Let me show you something," Seren said, pulling a hot poker from the crackling fire along the adjacent wall. Hannah sat up, not sure what to expect.

Seren strung the keys Hannah had given her onto a metal circle and hooked it on the end of a poker, placing it back into the fire. "I know just the thing. Tell me your intention and it will be so."

Hannah searched in her soul for the answer. "May the keys unlock the hidden mysteries whilst removing the afflictions I suffer."

"Díghlasáil an rúndiamhair,

Bhaint as an ngalar."

Seren said as she stared into the fire.

"Unlock the mystery,

Remove the dis-ease."

Hannah watched and remained quiet.

Seren then took the poker from the fire and held it in front of her, the keys glowing a bright orange like hot lava. She walked toward a large marble table in the middle of the room and placed the glowing keys upon a black metal plate. After placing the poker back in the fire, she returned to the table and stood over the keys. She closed her eyes and stood in silence. Hannah watched and waited, not wanting to disturb the process. Eventually she noticed that the keys were moving slightly, beginning to change shape on their own and gradually liquifying into a small shiny puddle.

She thought about the time she had been sick as a child. Her grandmother had accidentally dropped the thermometer, broken the glass and launched into a panic about the small pool of mercury on the floor, telling her not to touch it. But Hannah's eyes had fixed on the thick, shiny liquid in fascination.

She felt that same captivation now, watching Seren.

"This is the beginning of my tincture for you."

"How did you do that?" Hannah asked in amazement. "The metal turned to liquid, but you didn't touch it."

"The best way I can describe it is that I am a metal midwife. My family are descendants of metallurgical mysticism. As alchemists, we have the ability to commune with the elements and transform creation."

"So, you can bend metal...with your mind?" Hannah asked.

"Essentially, yes. My family were also truly blacksmiths, but that was simply because it helped us blend into the world. We really didn't need hammers and anvils. They just explained the end product we were able to produce. Over time, they discovered that the forge helped them stay grounded in this reality, and it became the family trade. PK, some call it, short for psychokinesis. We can move metal with our minds."

"That is amazing," Hannah exclaimed. "I wonder why Ashlin didn't tell me all this."

Seren smiled. "Some things are best understood firsthand. We combine PK with metallurgy; it is our alchemical calling. Our traditions are as old as fire itself, but they were misunderstood. We hid them over time."

"You weren't the only one," Hannah said, realizing that Seren was a descendant of one of the Seven Sisters.

"Eventually, my ancestors decided it was best to separate themselves from society to preserve the traditions, so they came here to Maple Hollow with other families that felt the same. Yours included." Seren smiled at her.

Hannah began to wonder if Seren knew of the curse, too. It seemed that everyone did, except her.

"Our abilities have evolved over generations, and now I carry on the tradition by offering metallurgical healing to those who find me."

"That's fascinating. I've heard of blacksmiths in the olden days, and I've heard of alchemists. But I never thought about the two going together. And I certainly never met anyone whose trade was either," Hannah said.

"Since you were led to me, you were meant to discover this. I don't reveal it to everyone, only those whose spiritual calling will benefit. There is great healing in metals, and we have been gifted with the ability not only to interact with them in a unique way, but to metamorphosize them into healing conduits, transferring healing to the physical body from the spiritual realm."

Hannah heard the word "healing" and a note of hope rose in her heart. Seren's family were Healers of the Hollow, too. They were working together.

"I had no idea. I'm honored to meet another healer. And I'm so glad I found you," Hannah said.

"I am honored as well. Your family has just as illustrious of a history. We all have our own paths, but they are intertwined in many ways. Each one of us has unique abilities that, when combined, form a powerful alliance. Each one of the families has passed down powers that are significant, can overlap, and can also benefit each other."

Seren walked to a nearby shelf, fetched a vial, and returned to the table. She poured the metallic substance into the vial, the glowing silvery liquid sliding down the inside.

"Return in three sunsets and I shall have your elixir," then she disappeared behind the chimney, the little wolf scampering behind her.

***

When Hannah got ready for bed that night, she replayed the events of the day in her mind. Seren had been one of the most unusual people she had ever met in Maple Hollow—and that was saying something. Hannah was fascinated, not only with the forge, but also with her kitchen. And little Liraen had been such a peculiar cat. Even out of all the cats at the lounge, she'd never seen one like her.

She tucked herself under the sheets and blankets, fluffed her pillow, and prompted Midnight to join her in bed. When she drifted off to sleep, she dreamt she was at a craft fair. In a sense, it was a bit similar to a street fair on the island, but in other ways, it was quite different. Hannah held in her hand a map, but despite her attempts to examine it, its logic eluded her. Although she had arrived with her parents, she was going to see her friend who was working at the fair. As she approached the table, she noticed her friend was working on an unusual machine that appeared to spin thin, baby blue yarn on a circular reel into a big bundle.

On the street, Hannah saw large buses and crowds of people who were boarding them, discussing amongst themselves that they were going home. A man approached her and said, "Just use your card. It will take you right past the island," as if that was the way home. He stood there waiting for Hannah to nod in acknowledgment. "For when you are ready," he said, bowing and walking away.

When Hannah woke up, she grabbed her dream journal, nearly knocking everything else off the nightstand as she passed her sleepy hands over it, grasping for her pen. She wrote down what she could remember. The craft fair, but it wasn't Maple Hollow. Was it a place she had been before? Or did it remind her of somewhere she'd been? The main objects were the map and the yarn machine. There was her friend, the man who approached her on the street, and all the people that were boarding the bus.

Lastly, there was the card. Well, she hadn't been handed a card, but the man seemed to imply she already had one. That she could obviously use and wasn't. *What was beyond the island, if she were to go past it?*

She thought more about her friend at the fair. Immediately, she could see the wordplay and irony in the term "spin yarn," because spinning yarn was a euphemism for telling a tale. But was it a false tale or just an imaginative one? Her friend seemed proud of her invention. The vibrant blue color of the yarn faded in Hannah's mind's eye as she grasped for the images of the dream.

When she had seen the people boarding the bus, she'd felt unsure if she should join them, and even questioned if she could. But there was encouragement from the strangers in her dream to find her way. To decipher the map she held in her possession. To use her "card." Could that refer to her abilities, the ones Seren spoke of, that all female descendants of the Seven Sisters had?

Was this telling her she had all she needed to discover? Was she just doubting her own ability again? Was the friend in the story really just an aspect of herself, encouraging her to be inventive, industrious, and set her own direction?

Hannah felt that her dream, like others before it, was trying to send her the message that she was ready for the challenge she faced. Perhaps she was somehow already equipped with what she needed and she just needed to remember.

CHAPTER EIGHTEEN

THE HOLLOW

OCTOBER 29, 2013

H annah awoke suddenly. She could see beyond her eye mask that the morning light was starting to peak through the fabric of the curtains, glowing around the frame of the window from outside. Tomorrow was the first day of the Halloween Hollow, a three-day event from sundown on the 30th to sundown on November 1st. Hannah had agreed to help Morgan get Maple Moon ready for the tourists. After Hannah rescued Merlin and Milu several years before, Morgan had made Hannah part owner of the shop, and she usually spent several afternoons a week helping her source magickal inventory.

Thoughts of her craft fair dream swirled in her mind as she leisurely walked to town. She wasn't in a hurry and wanted to take in all the sights. The sky was a light blue with lots of puffy white clouds. Golden leaves shimmered on the trees as if they were waving at her, while bright red and orange ones fell to her feet and crunched as she walked. The birds actively chirped multiple tones and sounds, speaking to each other from tree to tree while bright, multi-colored monarch butterflies flapped their wings, dancing amongst the falling leaves. She walked past shops with entrances graced by gathered urns, gourds, straw, and bundled flowers bursting out of wooden barrels. Shiny, bright orange pumpkins were haphazardly placed all along the winding cobblestone sidewalks.

When she arrived at Maple Moon, Morgan greeted her at the door. "Well, hello! I've got your day all planned out for you."

She wanted to tell Morgan about the prophecy and the riddles, but she sensed it wasn't the right moment. "Good morning! What would you like me to do first?" she asked, setting down her travel mug on a small open spot on the table amongst various fair fliers.

"Can you be a dear and go see who needs help setting up their booths outside?"

"Of course," Hannah said, grabbing clips, tape, and stakes and heading back out.

There was a small gathering of women unloading storage boxes and tents from their cars. Hannah walked toward them, waving her hand in welcome.

"Good morning! I'm Hannah from Maple Moon. Can I give you a hand?" she asked, holding out her arms.

"That would be great," said a short, stocky older woman with speckled gray hair. As she passed a box to Hannah, their fingertips touched, and the woman stared up at Hannah in a daze. "You have a block, you poor thing," she said, stopping her unpacking.

"A block?" Hannah asked, not sure what she was talking about.

"Your energy centers—they are not all free. Come here for a moment." The woman led Hannah to sit on a small folding chair under the tent. "Do you mind if I give you a reading?" she asked first, making sure she wasn't overstepping by offering her analysis.

"Not at all," Hannah said, making herself as comfortable as she could.

"Very well then. Close your eyes. Let your thoughts float upon the breeze and away from the hustle and bustle around us."

Hannah obliged.

The energy reader began breathing deeply to center herself. Then she sat in silence once more.

"You may now open your eyes," she instructed, placing her hand on Hannah's knee.

"There are seven main chakras, and many more depending on who you ask," she began. "Each one can be thought of as an energetic spiral, which to operate correctly needs to spin unencumbered. I did a scan of your etheric body from your feet up, and although your bottom three chakras are operating correctly, I encountered a block once I got to the top four." The woman stood back up and returned to her unpacking.

"Etheric body?" Hannah repeated. That is what Ashlin had suggested was the location of her dis-ease. "A block? What does that mean?"

"My guides were making me feel a sort of resentment feeling. Resentment about being abandoned. Does that resonate?"

Hannah's jaw dropped open. She wasn't exactly ready for this type of revelation. She did have resentment, deep inside her. When her parents had died, she felt like they had abandoned her. Then her grandmother, who she lived with, passed. Both things were out of her control. She didn't want to feel this way toward her family, but she did. There was truth in what the woman had sensed. Hannah wondered how she could transmute her feelings and cross the threshold to a place beyond her sorrow.

"Yes...I think I know what that's about," she said aloud, with some avoidance. She was unsure how to resolve the feelings that were being unearthed.

"Good. How you heal this is entirely up to you. I'm hearing from my guides that you are on the path to becoming a great spiritual teacher. But you think that requires that you obtain infinite amounts of knowledge—it does not. What it *does* require is that you open your heart to the messages you receive. Take time to reflect on it, and the answers will come."

As Hannah rose from her chair, she noticed the tent was beginning to be surrounded by milling tourists, ready to do their shopping. Then, through the crowd, she saw a tall man standing across the street. There was something familiar that she couldn't place. She quickly stepped inside the Maple Moon. He wasn't shopping. He was staring at her.

CHAPTER NINETEEN

THE GRIMOIRE

Hannah found Morgan sitting near the fireplace on a small loveseat, holding a stick with a small feather on the end and playing with her gray cat, Merlin.

"Hello dear, come sit!" Morgan said, patting the fabric, offering a space to Hannah next to her. "We need a moment of respite before we start the hard work."

"You look cozy," Hannah said as she took her place next to Morgan. Her eyes were fixed on the fire. She finally had a chance to talk to her, but she wasn't sure where to start. "I've been meaning to tell you about a ritual I did with Ashlin last Thursday," she finally blurted.

"Do tell, dear. What happened?" Morgan listened patiently.

"It was a mirror ritual. When we called in the ancestors, seven spirals appeared in the sand on the mirror. And then we saw letters forming a prophecy. It started out with

Seven Moons, Seven Suns, Sisters of Skye, We are One."

"Sisters of Skye?!" Morgan exclaimed, her eyes wide but continuing to play with Merlin.

"Then it said *I Separate but Also Allow, I Stand in Silence Until You Know How, With Just a Twist, Reveal the Unseen, Access the Timeline in Between.* It went on: *Seven Riddles Precede the Shadow Hour, Gather the Keys of our Legacy Power—*"

"Seven Riddles?" Morgan interrupted.

"Yes. I've started to receive them in my dreams. Well, the first three anyway."

"And what else?"

"The last lines are concerning: *Unlock the Crossroads under the Darkest Skies, Or Within This Room Meet Your Demise.*"

"Hm, crossroads. Like intersections? What if it's not literal, not streets, but invisible convergence?" Morgan speculated.

"Like ley lines?" Hannah offered.

"Yes, exactly. And what room?" Morgan asked.

"We were in a high turret at the manor, so in there, I suppose," Hannah explained.

Before Morgan could respond, her black cat Milu came scampering into the room chasing Merlin. Merlin jumped up on a side table to escape, but Milu jumped onto the bookshelf behind it. They were standing on their back paws with their front paws in the air, swinging at each other in play. Milu lunged off the bookshelf and it started to teeter back and forth, and then came crashing down onto the side table, books flying everywhere.

"Watch out, dear!" Morgan said as they quickly jumped off the loveseat. "Oh my, just what I need today."

"Let me help you." After assisting Morgan to right the bookshelf, Hannah started picking up the scattered books and stacking them into a pile. "This one's beautiful," she said, reaching under the table to grab a large, dusty volume.

"What is it?" Morgan asked, lifting it up to the light.

"It must have been on top of the bookshelf," Hannah surmised in an unsure tone.

Then she caught her breath. "I have been looking for this for ages." Her hands were trembling. "This is part of the island's legacy, *Grimoire de Hollow*! I always hoped to find this, and it was right here under my nose the whole time. I can't believe it!" Her tone shifted from caution to excitement.

"Really?" Hannah was becoming equally excited.

"So much powerful wisdom." Morgan flipped the pages quickly to and fro. "This was passed down through many generations. I was told tales of it as a child by my mother, but thought it was lost to the passage of time. I'm not even sure how it came to be here at Maple Moon, but it found you!"

"You mean...I didn't find it, it found me?"

"Yes, exactly. Books find those that need them, when they are ready to receive their message. They too have their own minds and energy."

Hannah sat down in her chair and realized this description perfectly explained why she and Ashlin were able to commune with books, since books truly had their own spiritual existence.

"I've gone this long without it, I can wait a little longer. It's yours now to discover," Morgan said, placing the book in Hannah's lap. "Everything happens for a reason, and its secrets are calling for you. I'm sure you will return it when it is time."

"Thank you, Morgan. I'm honored to receive it." Hannah grasped the book in her hands, wondering if it could help her unravel the riddles and protect her from the fate foretold in the prophecy.

Chapter Twenty

THE COMMUNING

That evening, after she and Morgan had closed up the shop and grabbed a bite to eat together, Hannah hurried along the sidewalk to the Maple Hollow Library to meet Ashlin. Even though she was tired, and worried about the message she'd received from the energy reader, she was eager to tell Ashlin what had happened with Seren.

During the day, the library was open to the public, but at night, when it was closed, Hannah and Ashlin could meet under the cover of darkness. Ever since Hannah had learned from Ashlin how to commune with books, they had bonded over their shared magick and found solace in each other's company. They would regularly meet amongst the stacks at night and spend time delving into tomes of ancient wisdom.

When she arrived at the library, Hannah went around to the back entrance; Ashlin had given her a key. This arrangement also kept their magickal meetings more private. Not that anyone in town would question clandestine midnight meetings in Maple Hollow, but it did make things easier.

"Ashlin?" Hannah called as she entered the back door and walked down a short dark hallway toward a larger room filled with books.

"In here, Hannah," Ashlin called back. Hannah followed the sound of her voice.

When she entered the room, she saw Ashlin standing on a tall floor-to-ceiling ladder, her slender legs dusted by her long skirt, her bare feet teetering on the top step as she stretched toward a large volume that was barely out of reach. The entire room glowed with a golden hue from the dancing flames of the candles atop five candelabras, arranged in a circle.

"Sorry I'm late," Hannah said as Ashlin descended the ladder and walked toward her. "I was helping Morgan get ready for tomorrow and forgot what time it was."

"You're just in time," Ashlin said, greeting her with a warm embrace, although Hannah suspected she was contemplating how unusual it was for her to be forgetful. The wide neckline of Ashlin's shirt exposed her bare shoulder, her hair gently tousling down the side of her face. "Did you get a hold of Seren?" she asked.

"I did! Thank you for the referral. You didn't tell me she was an ancestral alchemist and a Healer of the Hollow! She's preparing something for me that will be ready on Halloween night."

"I knew you would figure it out," Ashlin said, smiling. "So, what's the plan tonight?" she asked, shifting her gaze to the book Hannah held in her hands.

"Tonight, I have a very special book for us."

"Oh, I'm excited. What is it?"

"It's a surprise, but you'll see how it all adds up," Hannah said coyly.

"You always pick the best ones," Ashlin said, touching her shoulder and then dropping her hand to caress the engraving on the volume. They stood in silence, inhaling the scent of the pages. That unmistakable old book smell they both loved mixed with the scent of melted wax and slightly burnt wicks.

"Will you place it in the circle? I'll be right back," Ashlin disappeared momentarily.

"Of course." Hannah spun around toward the circle of candles placed on the ground. But as she turned, her equilibrium shifted and her balance with it. She suddenly felt as if the room was moving slightly on its own, instead of her, and she grabbed onto the sliding ladder to stabilize herself. She wondered if this was similar to what had happened to her in the tunnels.

Ashlin had disappeared to the kitchen but quickly returned, holding a large decanter filled with a deep red liquid in one hand and two earthenware goblets in the other. "Here we go, now we're ready," she said with satisfaction, placing them on a small table between them.

"Let us begin," Hannah said in a gentle tone, shaking off her dizziness as she joined Ashlin inside the circle. She began to call in the directions, the ancestors, and their guides. Then they sat with the large volume between them. They raised their hands above it. A moment or two passed, and then Hannah spoke first, her eyes still closed.

"Cold as the Winter Branch
Warm as the Summer Sun."
Ashlin spoke next:
"Count the Bridge of Autumn
To be an Enlightened One."

They both opened their eyes in surprise. They had delivered the next riddle, but it was not in a dream this time, nor in another's voice. This one had to be different.

Hannah's thoughts first went to the mention of the seasons. Winter and summer didn't exist in Maple Hollow, a place of eternal autumn. What was the "bridge"? Even though she was on an island surrounded by sea, she didn't remember ever seeing a bridge, not over water anyway. The only access to Maple Hollow was by ferry. And how could a bridge be counted?

Their ritual continued. After finally closing the circle, Hannah and Ashlin parted ways, exchanging looks of curiosity and knowing while promising each other to think about the riddle and compare notes.

***

Once back at the manor, Hannah climbed into bed with the *Grimoire de Hollow*. But before long, she couldn't keep her eyes open. The weight of her eyelids fought her will to stay awake and read, but eventually she succumbed and fell into a deep sleep.

Inside her dream, Hannah was sitting in the parlor of the manor, playing the grand piano. As she gently twinkled the keys, she felt a presence just behind her. Suddenly the weight was redistributed on the bench as a small, furry gray tabby cat hopped onto it from the ground.

"Wixby!" Hannah said, delighted. She had not been visited by her dream spirit guide, who had lived his earthly life with Jewelia, in quite a while. "I was hoping my playing would call you in."

"I was sent by the other cats!" Wixby said matter-of-factly.

"Who? Nutmeg? Midnight? Lirean?" Hannah asked, and he sheepishly nodded, not specifying.

"What do you know about riddles?" she asked next, gently scratching his neck.

"I love riddles!" Wixby proclaimed.

"Good, because I have some I need help with!" Hannah began to recount the four riddles she'd received so far. She also told Wixby about the prophecy, the masked man at the Masquerade Ball, the tunnels, the solar flares, and the compass clock. "When you first discovered you could time travel in the pumpkin, and saw Jewelia when she was young, what do you think caused it to happen? Was it on Halloween?" she asked. Morgan had been the first to teach her about pumpkins as portals that could transport cats through time and space. And Halloween is known as a moment in-between time, when the veil is thinnest.

Wixby smushed up his face, twisting his whiskers in a grimace. "I guess it must have been the lightning?" he pondered.

"I *was* able to harness lightning to defeat the Illusionix. If I was trying to access a timeline outside of my own, or travel between timelines, how would I do it?" she asked.

"You'd need a big pumpkin," the cat joked, flipping his tail.

"Is there another way?" she persisted.

Wixby twisted his whiskers with his paw. "All you should have to do is find the crossroads."

"Crossroads of time?" Hannah said quickly, echoing Wixby's suggestion and remembering the prophecy. "At the...shadow hour?" she added.

Wixby didn't answer her directly. "Remember when you figured out how to read Jewelia's letter?"

"Yes, it was Midnight."

"Not who, but what" Wixby asserted coyly in a riddle sort of way, echoing what Hannah had said to Ashlin about the solar flares notification.

Hannah paused in confusion. The cat tilted his head as if Hannah was still not getting it.

"Look to the sky, then you'll know why," he finally said, jumping off the bench and running away.

Chapter Twenty-One

THE NUMBERS

Hannah woke up with a start and grabbed her dream journal. Wixby had never led her astray. He helped her every time she was stuck or couldn't find her way out of a puzzle. This time was no different. She knew he had appeared in order to help her, if only she could decipher how. What was it he had said? Something about the crossroads.

Then the memory manifested in her mind of the cryptic letter she had received from Jewelia years ago, the letter that told her she was part of the legacy of magick in Maple Hollow. Midnight had brought her a match, inspiring her to light a candle and hold it behind the parchment letter as she looked at it backwards in the mirror. This had unraveled the cryptic order of the letters, broken the spell, and allowed her to read it.

"Midnight!" Hannah said out loud.

The cat, sleeping quietly at her feet, raised his head with a jerk, his eyes startled and wide.

"Oh sorry, Midnight, not you," she said, petting his head in reassurance. "It's the time! Twelve midnight! That's why Wixby was trying to remind me of you.

That's when the crossroads will manifest, to be un-locked. And that's what the shadow hour means in the prophecy. I was thinking it had to be a shadow cast by the sun," she explained to the cat. "But mid-night is the darkest hour and the time of the darkest skies. That's the time the compass clock is stopped at. But what night? It must be on Halloween," she told the cat. "That's seven days from when we re-ceived the prophecy."

Midnight reached out his arm, stretching, and revealed his claws, then set his head back down on his paws to continue his nap.

"That's the in-between time. But how can I time travel like Wixby?" Hannah rhetorically asked the cat. "I certainly am not small enough to fit in a pumpkin."

She squished up her face in a grimace like Wix-by had, trying to think. She was starting to feel closer to solving the riddles she'd received thus far. She felt fairly confident about several of them: having escaped being trapped in the underground tunnels, being reunited with her grandfather's com-pass, and now Seren was concocting her healing elixir. Progress was slow but steady.

Then again, there was only one midnight left until Halloween night. Maybe the crossroads would appear on the 30th? She was supposed to go to the art exhibit at the Whispering Whiskers to kick off the Halloween Hollow. What if whoever had stalked her in the tunnels was there? What if the masked man who had showed up at the Masquerade Ball and her energy reading was there? Hannah's feelings of reassurance from the dream with Wixby quickly started to fade the more she thought about it. Whoever seemed to be watching and pursuing her, they were still out there and would likely return. She didn't have much time left.

***

After breakfast, Hannah ducked into the library to look for a book on numerology. Part of her felt there was significance to the riddle's reference to counting. She climbed the rolling ladder and scanned the highest shelves, eventually finding an old dusty volume, *Divining with Digits*.

After getting comfortable in her favorite chair, Hannah placed the book in her lap, closed her eyes, and held her hands out. She began to commune with the book, transferring all of the knowledge of the mystical patterns of numbers into her mind.

When she opened her eyes, she had a startling realization, and her mind began churning with all the information she had consumed. Immediately she began to add up the numbers of the date her parents had died. It was October 17, 1987. She added together 1,0,1,7,1,9,8,7. It equaled 34, and once the three was added to the four, it equaled seven.

The book had told her that the number seven represents both sides of wisdom, both intuitive and calculated. She knew it was no coincidence that those who feel a strong connection to dates that numerologically equal seven tend to be highly driven to solve mysteries. The energy of the number seven calls to spiritually dive into introspection, to discover hidden meaning.

This couldn't be more true, Hannah thought as she felt a wave of validation. "The number seven represents a quest for truth," she said out loud.

She felt a flash of inspiration. Even the date of their accident was screaming at her to uncover the truth. She was a seeker and always had been. The patterns of synchronicity had followed her continually since that day. It was no coincidence that she had freed her aunt from dream captivity with the resonance of the musical scale, which contained seven notes. Nor that she had seen a moonbow of seven colors in her dream years ago after destroying the Illusionix. And the women who founded Maple Hollow, well there were seven of them, of course!

Hannah couldn't resist. She began to wonder if she could calculate the numerology of her name. No sooner than she asked, the book flipped open to a page that detailed an ancient cipher code that assigned a numerical value to each vowel. Calculating for her name, H and N were part of a grouping for number 5, and A for number 1. Hannah then was 5, 1, 5, 5, 1, 5, and Skye was 3, 2, 1, and 5. All combined, the numbers of her first and last name, equaled 33, her master number. Further broken down, 3+3 equaled 6.

A smile widened on her face as she read, *33/6 means Healer*.

"Unbelievable," she said aloud, once again rousing the attention of Midnight, who was quietly sleeping in the sun on the window nearby. He raised his head slowly with eyes half open as if to say, "Do I have to get up?"

As she continued reading, the next paragraph explained that in addition to a master number, there was also a soul urge number, which represented her deepest heart's desire, the culmination of all that motivated her on the inner plane. She nearly fell off her chair as she calculated...it was seven!

This not only meant that she had a deep desire for spiritual seeking, introspection, and discovering enlightenment through her intuition and extrasensory perception, but seven was also the numerologically significant number of the day she lost her beloved parents. The number in the prophecy, and the number that had shaped her ancestry, were the same, and it was not a coincidence.

CHAPTER TWENTY-TWO

THE STONES

OCTOBER 30, 2013

The streets of Maple Hollow were bustling with tourists partaking in Halloween activities. Gathering clouds swept across the sky. Hannah popped into Maple Moon, a new question on her mind. She waited while Morgan finished up with a customer and then quickly walked over to her.

"Morgan, I've been meaning to ask you about something. Do you know what these stones are?" From her pocket, she produced the crystal-looking stones she had found in the tunnel.

"Where did you find these?" Morgan said enthusiastically.

"Oh, I can't believe I forgot to tell you. The day after the prophecy, when I was leaving work, I found an underground tunnel between the Whispering Whiskers and the manor. It was pretty scary and I ended up fainting, I think. The stones were down there."

"A tunnel! Well, my dear, these are Clear Quartz. These stones work as amplifiers, guiding one to the inner realms, fostering intuition and aiding in the discovery of one's true spiritual path. They are particularly beneficial to the throat chakra, helping to nurture communication, release emotions, and encourage lucid dreams."

"I actually had a lucid dream right after I found them!" Hannah shared with surprise, while thinking about her energy reading the day before.

Morgan smiled and reached for another, rolling it between her fingers. "Ah, the master healer. In ancient times, they were used to make crystal balls for divination. The Egyptians highly regarded these stones as sacred. In modern times, they're actually used in radios, clocks, and even underwater echolocation. They raise your vibration as well as serve as protection, deflecting negative energy and intent. Perhaps it is why you made it home unscathed."

"The stones protected me? Clocks and radios? I never knew that! " Hannah asked, surprised. She extended her hand as Morgan returned them to her palm.

"That and so much more. It was no coincidence you discovered these. In fact, I think that they found you. They came to you in your moment of need. I have something else that will compliment these well." She walked toward one of the floor-to-ceiling bookshelves against the wall. "Here we are," she said, coming back with a small, clear glass bowl full of colorful stones that she put on the small table between them. "This is Kyanite. It is formed by a process called metamorphism under high pressure. Pick one."

Hannah dipped her fingers into the bowl, touching the jagged rocks. Like metallic blades, they were deep blue and green.

"These are beautiful. What do these do?" she asked, taking one from the bowl and holding it in her hand.

"These are portals between realms, conduits to other dimensions, giving you access to universal wisdom. Kyanite helps us solve problems through our dreams, clearing out our energy centers and allowing for one's universal consciousness to flow through."

"Energy centers...like chakras?" she asked.

"Ah, the chakras, the vortexes of our consciousness," Morgan replied. "Yes, well, there are many more than seven, but seven main ones. Starting from the base of one's spine up to the crown of one's head, they are Root, Sacral, Solar Plexus, Heart, Throat, Third Eye, and Crown. And beyond those seven, there is an eighth, the Soul Star."

Hannah continued to gaze at the stones. "I'm wondering if there is a connection between the Seven Sisters of Skye and the seven chakras. More specifically, if the seven riddles are maybe the 'keys' that the prophecy wants me to gather. Keys that relate to each chakra."

"That is very intuitive of you, dear! I can see how the sisters could have used that system to encode their secrets, allowing only those who had fully done the work to clear their energy to obtain the knowledge. Did you tell me that you and Ashlin saw spirals in the sand during your ritual?"

"Yes, seven spirals," Hannah confirmed.

"The chakras are oftentimes represented as circular spirals of energy. When they are blocked, they cannot spin, but once unfettered, they are much like a pinwheel, continually rotating within."

"Spirals? Blocked?" Hannah said, thinking of the parchment from the compass clock but also remembering what the energy reader had told her. "A woman setting up her tent yesterday gave me a rather impromptu energy reading while I was outside. She said my bottom three chakras were clear, but that once she scanned toward the upper half of my body, there was a block."

"The fourth chakra would be your heart, my dear."

Hannah thought back to the second riddle:

A Closed Hand Cannot Receive

A Distrusting Heart Cannot Relieve

Was she, herself, the one with the distrusting heart? Were her hands closed? If so, how could she open her heart to receive?

At that moment Milu came bounding up from the back of the shop, and shortly after, in hot pursuit, was Merlin.

"How can I open my heart?" she asked Morgan after the ruckus subsided.

"Ah, there are many ways. Let's start here," Morgan said, passing a Rose Quartz to Hannah. Then she reached for a small singing bowl and struck the edge with a mallet.

"What's that frequency?" Hannah asked. She remembered how she had discovered the healing frequencies of sound several years ago in her quest to free Jewelia.

"This one is 639 Hz. It's tuned to the heart. You can take this with you, along with these stones," she offered, passing the bowl to Hannah.

"Thank you so much," Hannah said, putting her stones in her pocket and grasping the vibrating bowl. Its resonance echoed within the room as it passed through her hands.

CHAPTER TWENTY-THREE

THE MIRROR

Hannah made her way home from Maple Moon to get ready for the art exhibit at the Whispering Whiskers. As she walked down the hallway toward her bedroom, she passed a spare room. No one was staying in it; in fact, there were many empty rooms at the manor, but it had a guest—once. It was the room where Wendy's guest, Jezebelle, had stayed during her visit to the manor. One day, while tending to her bedside with Jewelia, Hannah had noticed a picture on the wall. Her eyes were drawn to this same portrait now as she passed the doorway, and something called to her to stop and re-examine it once more.

Hannah walked toward the picture and stood in front of it, waiting to hear its whispers. In the photo, was a group of young women with their arms around each other's shoulders. She knew three of the women in the picture: Jewelia, Wendy, and Morgan. But she had never asked who the fourth woman was, and she didn't recognize her. In addition, in the background were two men. She hadn't noticed them before. She then also began to wonder who had captured the picture.

She took the frame off the wall and stared closer. To her surprise, she realized for the first time, one of the men in the photo was her father! His sandy brown hair and memorable smile now leaped off the page in recognition. How had she not seen him last time? And who was the other man? He was taller than her father with thick eyebrows, piercing eyes, and a tattoo she couldn't make out on his forearm.

It was a difficult yet wonderful time, Jewelia had said when Hannah had asked her about the picture. But she also remembered Jewelia saying, *That was the summer we came into our power.*

"Summer?!" she exclaimed out loud, the lightbulb veritably popping up above her head. "But there is no summer in Maple Hollow!"

She had always assumed the picture was taken on the manor grounds. That the sea behind them in the picture was the sea around the island. But she hadn't actually put it together until now...Maple Hollow had no summer. There were green trees in the background. That meant that the picture was taken somewhere else. Somewhere there *was* summer, but where? Why had Jewelia not mentioned it? And why had she not thought to ask?

She then remembered that Jewelia had also said, *When we discover something about ourselves, we aren't always ready to accept it.* She had always wanted to know what that time of her aunt's life was like.

She continued down the hallway, entered the bathroom, and started up a hot, steaming shower. When she stepped inside, the water crested the top of her head and cascaded down around her body. She stood in silence, inhaling the hot vapors and enjoying the warmth of the water around her. She always had amazing ideas while in the shower. There was something so transcendent about the experience, something so hard to replicate. She tried to remember her ideas by assembling small words together, like a cargo train waiting for departure. If she consolidated them into more easily portable thoughts, perhaps she could de-compartmentalize them upon arrival.

She always struggled to harness her light bulb moments; the ideas came easily and fluidly as the water ran down around her, but once she crossed the threshold out of the shower, it was as if they were wiped from her mind, her transition into the regular world closing the veil behind her.

Finally, it was time to get out. Hannah grabbed a towel and began to dry off her hair. As she tossed her head back and forth, that feeling of instability she'd experienced at the library returned. It was like she was on an amusement ride. Tomorrow morning, she would pick up her elixir from Seren. Hannah was counting down the minutes.

As always, her mind returned to the curse. Were her symptoms part of it? She could feel her health declining and worried whether she'd be able to fight the *Autonemesis Paradoxum* even with the help of the elixir.

When she stood back up, her mouth fell open as she stared into the mirror. In the fog, written upon the glass, was another riddle:

I Cannot Be Seen

I Can Only Be Heard

Shift Dark to Light

Embody the Spoken Word

Before Hannah could reach for her bathrobe, the lights in the bathroom flickered and then went out.

It was an overcast afternoon, storm clouds darkening the sky—no sunlight graced the room. Disoriented, Hannah quickly fumbled for the light switch. When it didn't work, she walked out into the long dark hallway.

"Jewelia? Wendy? Are you guys up here?" she yelled.

"We're down here, love," Jewelia finally answered, coming out of the kitchen with an oil lamp.

"It appears the power has gone out. I'll fetch Mr. Adams to check it out," Wendy yelled.

"Jewelia, please come quick. There's a message on the mirror!" Hannah called down the stairs. "It's the fifth riddle."

Jewelia moved swiftly up the stairs to Hannah. "Show me," she said. They entered the bathroom and Hannah pointed to the words on the glass.

"What could this mean?" Jewelia put her hands on the mirror to take a closer look. But the message was quickly disappearing.

They could hear Old Man Adams' voice echoing up from the foyer. "It *is* Mercury retrograde, so electric disturbances are common at a time like this," he was saying to Wendy.

"Let's go see what they found out." Jewelia motioned to Hannah to follow her back downstairs. Hannah grabbed her robe.

"Are we sure it's just a power outage?" she asked as they walked hand-in-hand down the steps. She pointed to the grandfather clock, whose arms had stopped. She pulled out her phone, and the time appeared to not have advanced there either. "The power shouldn't affect the clock, nor my phone!"

"Something else is going on," Jewelia drew in her breath sharply. "Someone is attempting to stop time!"

"Someone? Or something," Hannah said. "And now we have the next riddle."

"The curse," they said together, looking into each other's eyes.

CHAPTER TWENTY-FOUR

THE SUMMER

"You received another riddle? How?" Wendy asked as they reached the foyer. Hannah quickly recited the verse:

"I Cannot Be Seen
I Can Only Be Heard
Shift Dark to Light
Embody the Spoken Word."

They huddled at the foot of the grand staircase, comparing notes. "What can be heard but not seen?" Old Man Adams asked, raising his shoulders and holding his hands up in the air.

"Sound?" Jewelia said, raising an eyebrow.

"Yes, music," Hannah affirmed, thinking about the singing bowl that Morgan had given her at Maple Moon.

"But music is not 'the spoken word.' In fact, it's not spoken at all," Wendy interjected.

"Perhaps lyrics?" Jewelia said searchingly.

"Yes, I suppose singing would qualify. Maybe it has to do with both speaking and listening? Expression?" Hannah suggested.

"What do we speak with?" Wendy asked.

"Our mouth?" Old Man Adams answered.

"Our tongue?" Jewelia postulated.

"Our throat?" Hannah said third. Perhaps it was corresponding to the fifth chakra, which Morgan had explained rules both types of communications—spoken word and listening—being heard.

"Maybe you're supposed to sign something?" Wendy said, making sign language words with her hands.

"Or maybe it's reading someone's lips," Jewelia said.

"What if it's the voice, which you can't see, but it's delivered on a wavelength of sound, a frequency?" Hannah mused.

"Now you're onto something," Jewelia said, smiling. Morgan had told her that the Clear Quartz crystals were master healers which made radio transmissions and echolocation possible. Those could both be heard, but not seen. She began to wonder if the key to *this* riddle could be the stones she found in the tunnel.

"I think the curse is trying to stop us from deciphering the riddles. Slowing time and keeping us in the dark," she implored.

"I'll go check the breakers just to be sure," Old Man Adams said, excusing himself.

"Let's go back upstairs and get you dressed," Jewelia said, putting her arm around Hannah and walking her back upstairs.

"Hey, Jewelia?" Hannah stopped as they walked by the room with the picture.

"Yes, love?" she responded, sweeping Hannah's hair back across her shoulder.

"This photo." Hannah entered the room and walked toward the framed picture on the wall. "Who's in it again?" she asked, taking it down and handing it to Jewelia.

"Oh, you know. It's Morgan, Wendy, and me. Didn't we talk about it before?"

"Yes...but...who *else* is in the photo? Who is the other woman? I don't recognize her. And in the background, the two men?"

Jewelia hesitated. Hannah could see her demeanor change. Her hand holding the oil lamp began to shake a bit, and Hannah thought she could see her almost biting her lip in uncertainty.

"That, of course, is your father, love," passing the picture back to her.

"I thought so!" Hannah said with satisfaction.

"You're all wet, let's get you out of this soaking bathrobe," Jewelia said, turning to head toward the hallway.

"Why do I feel like there's something you're not telling me?" Hannah said directly, trusting her intuition.

Jewelia stopped mid-step, realizing there was no chance of avoiding the truth any longer.

"Okay, the only reason I have that picture up is because it's the only one of Morgan, Wendy, and me on vacation."

Hannah waited, curious about Jewelia's visible uneasiness.

"That other man with your father, his name was Zekerias. Trouble, he was," she remarked.

"Why was he trouble?" Hannah asked.

"That was many years ago, love. Some things are better left in the past."

"I'm just curious why I've never heard about him before," Hannah pressed.

"Well, they weren't friends for long, if that answers your question." Jewelia pieced out the information, still withholding bits.

"Why not?"

"We met him while on vacation. In retrospect, I realize it was foolish for us to leave Maple Hollow. We all thought it was harmless, a little fun."

"So, you traveled together?"

"We did. It was the only time we did something like that together. We met Zekerias and his girlfriend, Jaime. That's her there." She pointed to the girl on the left side of the group. "We got to talking and we ended up hanging out with each other the whole week."

"Sounds like fun," Hannah said, wishing she had siblings to vacation with.

"It was, until Zekerias got creepy. He started asking questions, really prying into where we lived and wanting to know details about our family. It was a bit strange. It made me uncomfortable, but your father didn't seem to notice. He wasn't always the best judge of character."

"Why would you think that?" Hannah asked, logically.

"Maybe he was a bit too trusting, if you know what I mean."

"Didn't you say that was the summer you and Morgan came into your power? How did you realize that? What happened?"

"Let's just say that we discovered what we were both capable of. But we weren't aware we had a secret observer."

"Zekerias?"

"Your father finally realized he was getting too inquisitive, and so we decided to end our trip early. We never saw him after that, thankfully."

"What do you think he wanted?"

"I don't know. I guess that's why I put it out of my mind. He made me uneasy, and I was glad to be back on the island. I haven't left since I realized how much we must protect our powers. There are others who want to possess them—and not for the good."

Hannah continued to stare into the photo, her mind swirling with so many other questions.

At that moment, the lights in the manor blazed to life.

Chapter Twenty-Five

THE EXHIBIT

Hannah was relieved to see that the dark clouds were breaking apart, sending shafts of the setting sun cutting through the trees as she biked to town. She arrived at Whispering Whiskers, eager to see Delvina's art exhibit and watch her performance. In keeping with the ancient Celtic tradition of guising to ward off evil spirits, all attendees were asked to conceal their identity by wearing masks.

Nutmeg came running up to Hannah as she moved through the lounge, meowing loudly.

"Well, hello, Nutmeg." Hannah bent over to pick her up, and the cat quickly obliged. As she held Nutmeg close and caressed her soft fur, she noticed how the vibration of the purr was filling her whole body. Nutmeg's fur was warm and soft, and Hannah suddenly felt a rush of emotion. The cat was perfectly present, perfectly soft, perfectly vibrating there in her arms. The vibration traveled through the air between their bodies and filled her heart with comfort. She suddenly realized that cats had always been the catalyst for this feeling. That she had always found solace in her relationships with them. They could provide something to her that humans could not. Their telepathic connection served as a conduit sending vibrational healing straight to her heart.

In the tunnel, Nutmeg had witnessed her fear and watched over her when she could no longer stand or breathe. She gently kissed the cat on her caramel-striped head, thanking her for reminding her of this truth and helping her on her journey to opening her heart.

After greeting the twins, Hannah poured herself a mulled cider from the refreshments table and took a seat close to the edge of the exhibit space. At each corner, stood white Corinthian columns as tall as the ceiling, like in her dream, wrapped in sparkly lights—shimmery dark fabric draped between them. The doors to the lounge opened. Tourists poured in, milling about, admiring the artwork hung on the walls, and waiting for the exclusive performance that was to come. It was sundown, and the Halloween Hollow was officially launched.

"Welcome, guests, to the most magickal art exhibit in Maple Hollow," Varlina announced, inviting the guests to gather around as she lowered the lights. A curious song began to play over the loudspeakers, ushering in an air of mystery and intrigue.

Hannah watched Delvina as she sat on the floor on a large drop cloth that extended around her for several feet. In the middle was a large canvas. The room that had been loudly bustling before, fell silent as all of the tourists stopped to observe the main event. The cats of the lounge, including Nutmeg, began to mill around almost frantically—their energy rising.

Delvina's eyes were closed, her breathing slow. It was as if she was moving her consciousness into a meditative state—a waking dream. In each hand, she held a long paintbrush. "Life is a canvas upon which I paint my dreams," she whispered under her breath.

At first, she was motionless. In front of her was a large rectangular palette, containing a long row of paint dollops of many colors. Suddenly, with her right hand, she dipped the brush into the paint and quickly began to spread it across the canvas.

Nutmeg darted toward the paint, dipped in her paw, and then shook it off, creating a splatter effect.

Delvina continued with her left hand. And another cat circled in, sniffing the various servings of paint for their selection, then dipping a paw into the palette, swiping up a bit of paint, and spattering it toward the showpiece.

The cats began to swarm around the painting, rolling on their sides, scratching their backs on the edge of the canvas and rubbing their faces onto it. They danced about, their paws in the air, as if an invisible force was tempting them.

Suddenly, Delvina was rapidly painting with both brushes on the canvas, to and fro, as if her arms were being orchestrated like a marionette attached to strings. Her eyes remained closed as the cats swarmed around taking turns with the paint, some of them standing on their hind legs as they reached across to make broad strokes.

Once Delvina had completed the transmission, her arms fell to her side. The paint dripped off the brushes onto the drop cloth. There was silence, and then an eruption of applause from the crowd. Delvina opened her eyes and observed what had been created.

Although the painting was abstract, when Hannah peered at the center of it, she saw definitive spirals in the midst of splatters from the cats' paws. She suddenly understood that the paint was a portal. Delvina's spontaneous artwork was like automatic writing—channeled from the beyond. And the cats were cosmic artists.

Everyone started milling about again, clamoring to purchase the paintings. Hannah noticed that one man in particular was extremely interested in Delvina's newest creation, gesturing to it and shaking wads of money. Varlina was shaking her head in refusal. Hannah began to wonder if it was the same man who had been staring at her at the Masquerade Ball. He was wearing a black suit and appeared to be about the same height. His dark curly hair was pulled back into a ponytail. Underneath his horned mask, she could detect sunken cheekbones and a thin face. Finally taking the hint, the man stormed out of the lounge.

Hannah crossed the room to see what was going on. "What was that about?" she asked Varlina.

"Oh, these tourists, you know..."

"Aren't you selling these paintings?"

"Not this one," Varlina nodded at the one on the drop cloth.

"Why not?"

"This one is for you," Delvina said, winking at Hannah as she approached.

Hannah felt speechless. "It's beautiful," she said, admiring the spirals and the cats' artistic prowess. "Oh, you guys, you didn't have to do this for me."

"The cats wanted to. Who am I to argue?" Delvina said, shrugging.

"They are all covered with paint now!" Hannah exclaimed.

"Ah, it's actually cat-friendly. Natural edible plant dyes spiked with catnip. They will happily clean it all off before morning."

"How clever," Hannah remarked.

"The paint does take a bit of time to dry. You can pick it up tomorrow and take it home," Varlina told her.

"Thank you both, this means a lot. It's spectacular," she said, giving them each a hug. A wave of sentimentality began to creep over Hannah. They were beginning to feel like family, while at the same time, it made her miss her own.

CHAPTER TWENTY-SIX

THE BOX

Seeing the old snapshot of Jewelia again and the legacy photographs in the Maple Hollow Theater, had filled Hannah with a sense of nostalgia. Now, back at the manor after the exhibit, she went into her bedroom closet and pulled out the box of memories that her grandmother had given her when her parents had passed. She revisited it from time to time, sifting through the pictures and newspaper clippings.

Her parents had gone out to dinner to celebrate their anniversary, and her grandmother had come over to watch her and stay the night. *Why were they taken from her? Why was she left behind?*

Hannah struck the singing bowl Morgan had gifted her. As the resonance filled the air, Hannah felt the feeling coming on that she always tried to avoid. But it was too strong this time, and she couldn't stop it. Her lips began to quiver, her jaw tightened, her heart started to pound. Then it hit. The tears started to stream down her face and full sobs filled the room. She handled it so well most of the time. But sometimes, something would set her off and the pain of losing her parents was just too much to bear. She had to release it. Let it flow through her. Yet once she did, she felt so much lower than before. It brought her so far down into the depths of sadness that she wasn't sure how she was going to find her way back up.

Even though many years had passed, it still pained her to think about. *What had happened in those final moments of her parents' demise? Did they have any time to reflect before the crash, or did it just all happen too fast? Had they crossed to the other side? What did they see when they did? Why could no one save them? And what caused them to go off the cliff in the first place?* All of these questions gnawed at Hannah's soul. She didn't believe what she'd been told and she never would until she found her own answers.

The emptiness filled her soul. She loved the community that surrounded her in Maple Hollow, but nothing had ever filled the hole in her heart left by the loss of her parents. The pain lessened with time, but it never fully went away. This time, she was overcome with it, enveloped in all-consuming sorrow. She felt a piercing sting in her heart and knew she could take no more.

Once she surrendered to the pain, the darkness rushed up from the depths to drown her. She thought about her dis-ease and all the struggles she was enduring with her own body. She collapsed on her bed in a flood of tears. The sides of her back tensed and spasmed as her heavy breath heaved. She surrendered to the hopelessness, the victimized feeling that had once been her default state, which she always tried so hard to rise above.

And now, she was grappling with this struggle within her own body. It was as if it was rebelling against her. It had a way it was supposed to work, but it wasn't. It had a pattern, a process, one that was designated in the halls of health as correct, and hers was not in compliance. Her body had somehow, for some reason, turned on her. *Autonemesis Paradoxum.* It had begun to attack itself, tearing down what she had tried to build, and leaving in its place a hollowed version of herself wondering what happened.

Some days, she would think everything was fine, going her daily way. But then other days, the universe would seemingly sneak up behind her and knock her down, disabling the function of one of her limbs, or perhaps an internal organ needed for survival. It could never be predicted, except the inevitableness that it would occur. Her normalcy could be jolted back into trauma at the drop of a hat. Her body, although it appeared to everyone around her as "normal" and "healthy," had evolved into something that was anything but. She had an invisible affliction, one that made her suffer in silence since no one could see it. But it was still there, festering underneath her skin. Hiding in the dark corners inside her physical self. Refusing to cooperate with her inner soul.

Hannah wondered why she had to suffer this way. And now that she was discovering the legacy of her ancestors, the Seven Sisters of Skye and the curse placed upon them, she realized that her question was not only relevant but completely valid. She didn't have to yield. She wasn't meant to succumb to it. Life could be easy. It could be okay to be happy, to be healthy, to be "normal," whatever she perceived that to be. But her family had been cursed. It was generational, stretching across the years, seeping into their bones and skin until they recognized it as part of their own DNA. But it was not part of them—it simply had been an unwelcome guest too long.

And now, with Seren's help, she would reverse it. Through the magick of alchemy, she would alter the suffering all the women in her family had fallen prey to, whatever form it had taken. Perhaps she could transform the invisible etheric afflictions into hidden powers. The things that had made them weak and vulnerable now would give them wisdom and ability beyond comprehension. All the descendants of the sisters would regenerate to super-human—disempowered to empowered. It was the reversal of all archaic opposites into an astonishing positive. The ancient oppressors would no longer have a hold. *Autonemesis Paradoxum* would be banished.

She had work to do before the shadow hour on Halloween night. Her legacy power was waiting for her and she just had to harness it. No one else would be meeting their demise in her timeline, even if she had to die trying.

Hannah ran out of her bedroom, fumbled with poor balance down the stairs, and rushed out the front door of the manor. Her face was immediately met with a fast rain, soaking her hair and clothes. She ran out onto the grass, shivering in her bones, the tears running as fast as the sheets of rain.

A bright flash of lightning lit up the sky and illuminated her path. She began to count. Seconds later, a loud boom of thunder cracked open the sky and rolled into the distance with all the rumble of a thousand armies.

She stared up into the sky, anger beginning to well up in her heart.

"Take me instead!" she yelled into the vast sky.

"Take ME!" she yelled again. Wishing if she somehow disappeared, perhaps her parents would reappear, blinked into this existence through a portal wormhole.

As she held up her hands to the air, her eyes staring up with helplessness, a shimmering ball of light appeared as if in answer to her request.

It appeared near the ground and erratically started to jump and encircle her. Small shoots of lightning emanated from its blindingly bright white center as it reached her hands. At first, she felt a blistering singe on her fingers, like she had touched a hot stove, but the heat quickly spread up her arms, hitting straight into her heart in a blast that shot right up out of her head, illuminating her whole body.

Hannah blacked out. All she saw was total darkness. Then there was no storm, no thunder, no lightning, no rain.

***

She slipped deeper and deeper into her subconscious. Her body became immobile.

She was at Lone Peak Cliff, standing on the edge, looking over. She reached into her pocket and pulled out her grandfather's compass clock. As she opened the top, the dial began to spin rapidly around, seeking direction. Her grasp began to grow weak. She could no longer hold it, her muscles atrophying and spasming. Her vision began to blur and she could no longer make out the directions on the dial nor tell which hour the clock arms pointed.

Then she heard a woman's voice. It was not one she recognized, nor had heard before:

Guides at Night
We Began as Twins
Where Duality Ends
A Third Begins

CHAPTER TWENTY-SEVEN

THE GREENHOUSE

When Hannah awoke, she was lying on the grass outside the manor in the dark. Her head was pounding, and her body was coursing with a strange surge of adrenaline. She stood up and wiped herself off. Not ready to go inside yet, she headed toward the greenhouse near the back door of the manor. She would often retreat there with Midnight to enjoy the scenery and rich scents. She was rarely in the greenhouse at night, but she remembered that yesterday, she had left the *Grimoire de Hollow* there.

As she entered, Hannah suddenly realized that the greenhouse was essentially an observatory, a veritable planetarium with its domed glass ceiling. As she stared up into the night sky, she mulled over possible explanations for the most recent riddle. What could *Guides at Night* be? Could this be about dream guides? She had encountered so many different guiding spirits since she came to Maple Hollow. She thought fondly of Abernathy, the tiny turtle who had brought her the silver key that enabled her to discover her powers in the dream space.

She had never put it together before, but ancient cultures considered turtles to be timekeepers. On their backs, they carried a complete calendar etched within their markings. He might have been trying to show her that time itself was one of the keys.

Then there were the owls, one of whom embodied a kaleidoscope, reflecting back the multi-dimensional aspects of herself. Leaf, who inspired her to remember and stay on course in finding the fabled Imni tree. And of course, Wixby, who had accidentally discovered how to time travel and helped her as she figured out how to rescue her aunt from the Dream Haunters.

Soon after arriving in Maple Hollow, searching for Jewelia after her desperate letter, Hannah had had a dream about a lighthouse, during which she'd found a compass in her pocket. And lighthouses were *Guides at Night.*

We Began as Twins. Delvina and Varlina were twins. But then she analyzed why the phrasing was "we began" as twins, as if they would no longer be twins in the future. Was something going to happen to one of the them? Could they be what the prophecy was about? And still, there was unsolved mystery of why there was a tunnel connected to the pumpkin patch.

Retrieving the volume from a bench, Hannah returned to the manor, contemplating the concept of duality. The moon and the sun could possibly be considered twins. They definitely were two parts of a whole—day and night. She began to brainstorm what other dualities might exist. Mind and body? Left and right? Good and evil? Male and female? Life and death? And what *Third* was beginning? If the duality was male and female, perhaps a child was the third?

Maybe she was the third, having begun from her parents, where duality ended?

Despite all she'd been through that day, Hannah was not sleepy at all. She went to her room and sat down with the book to commune. Raising her hands above it, she asked the pages for the answer to this conundrum of duality. The history of her family, and all the legends of the island, coursed into her mind.

Hannah felt her body lift, like the levitation in her dream. She remained calm and listened with her mind. Eventually she felt more grounded, and opened her eyes. "It's not just one curse, it's two." As she spoke, it was as if she was channeling answers from the beyond.

"First, all of the women ancestors who held power would suffer a great loss. The second aspect is one of personal destruction. The curse foretold that many women who possess power will suffer an illness that seeks to destroy the physical body, distracting them from their power and sapping them of their vitality. It attacks their bodies, enacting a slow destruction, so their power cannot be passed on, and is weakened in those who possess it."

She had asked for an answer, and the ball of lightning had revealed the next riddle. Her parents' and grandparents' sudden deaths were all due to the curse. And the weakening of her physical body she was experiencing, which was growing in intensity now, was due to the curse. Not only did it work to prevent any further offspring in the family line, through death or illness, but it was also set to weaken and destroy from the inside those who held the power. She was sick. Jewelia, years ago, was so weakened by Mercury retrograde that she had been unable to withstand the Dream Haunters.

"The curse! It's the Legacy Lock. It's up to me. My ancestors are all depending on me." Hannah sat very still. She had to clear her ancestral trauma and prevent further unnecessary death. She also had to heal herself—revitalize her cells that had fallen prey.

Hannah pulled her grandfather's compass clock from her pocket. Old Man Adams' words *it's right twice a day* echoed in her mind. The compass clock *was* correct at this moment: it was midnight, which meant it was now Halloween. The riddles, the celestial knowledge she had been acquiring, and Halloween...Samhain, the most sacred time of the year for the Celts...were so intricately connected. She placed her hands over the book once more and asked for the connection she was missing.

As she closed her eyes, looking with her third eye, and listening to the subtle whispers of the book's wisdom, she received the knowledge she sought. Halloween was actually an astronomical holiday itself. October 31st divided the light half and the dark half on the wheel of the year. Because this day ushered in the dark part of the year, it was considered by some to mark the start of the new year.

In addition, she learned about a unique astronomical event that occurred when a celestial body, whether it be a star, moon, or planet, reached its zenith, or highest point in the sky, at midnight. It was called the Midnight Culmination. And prior to the modern-day calendar, a very special one historically happened on Halloween—that of the Pleiades.

Observed when the veil between the worlds was thinnest, some ancient timekeepers even believed it signaled the end of the world, but that was merely a result of their limited understanding of death.

She'd had no idea there was a connection between Halloween and the Pleiades—her favorite holiday and the constellation she was the most fascinated by.

Feeling excitement rushing in her veins, Hannah opened her window and leaned out, looking up at the night sky. It was a deep, dark purple, yet brilliant and illustrious like a silky velvet blanket. Amongst the expansive starscape, she looked for the large constellation known as Orion, the Hunter. Her eyes followed the path of Orion's belt. Then out and beyond it, past the Aldebaran star. There she saw the cluster of bright blue stars, gathered together, that she always looked for.

It was the Pleiades, taking its throne at the zenith, the Seven Sisters assuming their reign high in the cross-quarter sky.

***

Sitting on her bed, Hannah reached for one of the Clear Quartz stones she had found in the tunnel. Holding it, she began to feel calmer than she had in days—despite the enormous task that lay in front of her. She held it in her hand and asked, in her mind's eye, to incubate a dream that would show her the seventh and, she assumed, final riddle. Now that it was technically Halloween, the time was almost up. She had to figure them out and fulfill the prophecy before midnight. Placing the stone under her pillow, she dipped one leg under the covers, then the other, nestling herself underneath.

Pulling the sheets up to her neck, she tucked the covers under her ears and closed her eyes. She tried to slow her breathing, to remain as still as possible to let her mind detach from her body. The onset of sleep was always such an elusive mystery to Hannah. It seemed there was absolutely no possible way for humans to will it. It had to evolve and happen out of sheer surrender and patience. Sleep would sneak up on her only once she was completely unaware and not paying attention, stealing her away beyond the cloak of consciousness. She had to wait for it, in silence, trusting it would eventually come.

When her brainwaves began to slowly transition from one state to the next, she finally drifted into sleep—ushered down the spiral of perception into realms beyond the manor.

She found herself in a place she didn't recognize, but there was something so familiar about it. It was a hotel room, the walls a deep purple burnout velvet. There were two large pianos. Snow fell softly outside a large picture window and a fire crackled in a corner fireplace. Hannah's eyes were drawn to a closed door. She perceived shadows lurking behind it, scraping at the wood. They were trying to get in.

She slowly approached. Her heart filled with trepidation. She felt hands pushing her from behind, as if she was in a crowded room of people all clamoring to get out. "We can't go yet," she tried to say in frustration to ease the pressure.

Then she saw a woman she thought she recognized, and her heart quickened in excitement. She smiled and waved. They embraced, and then she heard the woman's voice:

I Grow in the Garden

I Fill Up a Room
Faster Than Music
You Will Discover It Soon

CHAPTER TWENTY-EIGHT

THE ELIXIR

OCTOBER 31, 2013

Hannah awoke and scribbled the final riddle into her journal. As she became more awake, she remembered that not only had she embodied lightning the night before, but she'd finally grasped the nature of the curse and received the last riddle. Today was Halloween. Then she immediately thought about the two things she needed to pick up: the elixir from Seren and the painting from Delvina. It seemed like fate that they would both be ready now.

She heard her phone buzzing and looked down to see a text from Seren. Yes, in fact, the elixir was ready.

Hannah sent a quick reply that she would stop by before her shift at Maple Moon. It would be very busy in town, as it was the first full day of the traditional Halloween Hollow.

She headed to Seren's forge. As she slowly walked through the door, a chiming bell announced her arrival. The smell of charcoal, smoke, and burning embers wafted up to her nostrils as she stepped inside and closed the door behind her.

Seren emerged from the back, her large, dark apron scraping the floor. Liraen quickly scampered behind her, following her heels.

"Ah, there you are," she proclaimed. "It is ready," she said, waving her hand toward the kitchen door, bidding Hannah to enter. Hannah obliged, following her across the threshold.

"I have to admit, I'm a bit nervous," Hannah conceded.

"Listen to my words." Seren stopped walking abruptly. "You cannot hold fear and love in the same vibration. Love is the highest and fear is the lowest. You cannot proceed further while holding fear in your heart."

Hannah heeded her guidance, understanding that if she really wanted to heal herself, she had to open her mind and heart to that possibility. Seren's guidance brought to her mind the words of the second riddle:

A Closed Hand Cannot Receive

A Distrusting Heart Cannot Relieve

"I understand," she said, nodding.

Seren continued across the kitchen and returned holding a glittering vial of shimmering multi-colored liquid. Hannah's eyes widened. It appeared to be surrounded by a sparkling cloud.

"Is that..."

"Yes, these are your keys. I mixed in gemstone powders, transforming them into an elixir made only for you." She passed it to Hannah.

Hannah grasped the vial between her palms, continuing to stare at its wondrous colors, which danced in the light of the fire.

"Gemstones? Which ones?"

"I chose something called Firestone, named for its iridescent appearance."

"It's beautiful," Hannah said with admiration.

"Ah, it's much more than that. Otherwise known as Spectrolite, it is a strong spiritual protector."

Suddenly Hannah heard the riddle phrase *Face the Flames* in her mind. She began wondering if *this* could be what it was about.

"Warding off negativity, Firestone serves as a shield for the auric and etheric bodies while enhancing communication between the physical and non-physical realms," Seren continued. "Some have called it *the sanctuary of the stars* because it is believed to contain within it the aurora borealis."

"The Northern Lights? I saw them the other night for the first time! It was one of the most amazing experiences I've ever had," Hannah said, gazing at the magickal vial.

"It's brilliant, isn't it? I believe it brings galactic energies to our physical plane. It can awaken the third eye and serve as a catalyst for our inner vision," Seren explained.

"So, should I drink this now?"

Seren raised her hand. "Wait for the right time," she advised. "You will know when," she added, tapping her on the shoulder in reassurance. "For now, pay attention to the signs, as more will be revealed soon."

Hannah nodded, realizing she could not turn back now. "Will I see you tonight at the manor for our Silent Supper?"

"I'll be there!" Seren said.

Hannah graciously thanked the alchemist for creating the fiery elixir. She wasn't sure what consuming it would do, exactly, but she knew she had to proceed fearlessly. Fear had no place in her healing, and she had to embrace the unknown ahead to unlock her legacy and fulfill the prophecy.

***

Departing Seren's forge, Hannah walked along the quaint sidewalks of Maple Hollow toward the library. Ashlin saw Hannah enter and hurried to meet her.

"Hey, how are you?" she asked, reaching out to embrace her.

"Hopefully better soon! I just saw Seren," Hannah said. "You won't believe what's happened since the last time I saw you. I think I'm close to figuring things out!"

"Oh good! Come have a seat. I'm sure you'll be standing at work the rest of the day." She motioned for Hannah to join her on a small couch nestled amongst the stacks.

"I communed with the *Grimoire de Hollow* again."

"What did you find out?" Ashlin asked, leaning in with curiosity.

"It actually explains the whole curse that everyone has been telling me about. It's about the families of the seven women who first settled the island. The seven women's paths were so intertwined that they became known only as the Seven Sisters. These women were very powerful, but they were persecuted and not understood. Understandably, they sought refuge and created their own world in Maple Hollow, as we know."

"Right," Ashlin interjected. "What else?"

"They fiercely protected their beliefs, but they had to hide them, only communicating about them in riddles able to be unraveled by those with the sacred genetic knowledge necessary to decode them. But their persecutors continued to hunt them, seeking to obtain their power. The curse upon them locked up their powers, restricting them from developing. Although it didn't say who cursed them, or when. Now, their full powers can only be activated by decoding the riddles, gathering the elements that represent their powers, and unlocking something called the Legacy Lock. This is said to hold all of the secrets—the Secrets of the Seven Sisters of Skye." Hannah whispered this so the browsing tourists couldn't overhear.

"So, they really *were* the ones communicating with us in the ritual?" Ashlin said.

"I'm sure of it. Each woman had her own secret power. But they could all step across the veil into worlds unseen. As generations passed, they paired their powers to become synergistic, passing them down to all female descendants. I believe these are the "keys." Each one rules an aspect of reality—an energy center, if you will, like the chakras. But when combined, they become even more powerful."

"Did it explain the powers?" Ashlin leaned it closer.

"One woman's power was centered on the classical forces of the Earth: earth, air, fire, and water. A second woman's powers were concentrated on sound, and a third, on all creations of the sun—trees, rainbows, auroras, plants, and more. Those powers were representative of the elemental key, the frequency key, and the solar key. Then there was one who could alchemize metals by working with fire, and one who could speak to cats, recognizing their inter-dimensionality. Those being the mineral and the animal keys. Then there were the artistic ones, who wrote the literature, created the art, and blended edible aspects of Earth into culinary enchantments. This artistic key represented the superior knowledge of all creative and imaginative manifestations in the physical world."

"Elements, frequency, solar, minerals, animals, and the arts; that all makes sense," Ashlin concluded.

"Just like the legend goes, many moons ago, there was an island called Skye—the namesake for my family. It details the seven families: The Sironas, Seren's alchemical lineage and the Druantias, Morgan's legacy of the trees. Then there's Varlina's and Delvina's heritage, the Lanuarias, Wendy's culinary mastery of the Airmeithas, and your family, the Aldonas, the wisdom keepers. Like Morgan told me when I first came to Maple Hollow, each Healer of the Hollow had a different gift, but what I didn't realize until meeting with Seren, is that they were synergistic. Over time, these magickal abilities transferred to all women with this DNA in their veins. If they didn't live on the island, eventually they heard the call, like I did. That brought them home, and thereby home to their powers."

"So, even with the curse, the descendants still have remnants of their powers," Ashlin pondered.

"Remnants, yes. But not their full capacity. You, Morgan, Jewelia, Wendy, Seren, Delvina, and Varlina all embody combinations of these powers. Jewelia stewards the pumpkin patch and channels energy through the piano, these are the elemental earth realm and frequency keys combined. Morgan stewards the trees of the forest and all the creatures that live therein, including cats. This combines the solar and animal keys. Your power to commune with books while levitating is a synergy of the artistic and elemental air realm keys. Wendy's culinary prowess is a blending of the artistic and solar keys. Varlina founded the cat café which combines the animal and frequency keys. While Delvina holds a mixture of the artistic and elemental water realm keys, creating her lounge that showcases both piano music and her watercolor paintings." Hannah's voice trailed off as she looked at Ashlin.

"But that's only six, who is the seventh family?"

"I don't know anyone by this name, but the lineage diagram in the book says it's Danua."

"I don't recognize that either. Why are there no descendants left of the Danua family? What happened to them?"

"Good question, but I did discover that it was foretold one of the descendants would come to fully embody all powers of the Seven Sisters of Skye."

Ashlin sat back, taking it all in. Then she jumped to her feet. "You are the one, Hannah! You are the one our ancestors always dreamed of creating. It took many years, but now you exist, encompassing all that they embodied. You can commune with the pumpkins, you've divined by fire and water, you've harnessed lightning. Like Jewelia, you have the ability to wield sound frequencies for healing, and like Morgan, you're connected to creations of the sun: the flares, aurora, and the maple trees. You harness the power of stones to heal and enlighten. You share Varlina's connection to cats and my ability to commune with books."

Hannah sat motionless, feeling both shocked and honored. She knew. Had she always known? This knowledge both affirmed and explained the course her life had taken, in a way she could scarcely believe. And yet it all made sense!

She had experienced the pumpkin power firsthand, and called upon the other elemental forces of nature to assist in her works—like when she destroyed Norma Nyx by gazing at the fire. She had solved the mystery of frequency with the help of Wixby and discovered the fabled Imni tree along with the creatures of the forest, like Filgrim and Leaf. She had witnessed the energetic power of the aurora and solar flares, while also working with the guiding power of crystals and stones. Ashlin had taught her how to commune with books. Wendy had taught her the culinary arts. And the twins had not only provided a place for her to continue playing the piano, but also inspired her to further foster her unshakeable bonds with the cats of Maple Hollow. She had learned to do it all.

"Wait! We've only counted six powers," Ashlin suddenly exclaimed. "You must hold the answer to the final riddle, the final key, and thereby, the seventh power! If only we knew what the seventh family's power was."

Hannah knew that whatever it was, it was the last power she had to embrace deep within her. To reverse the clock and discover the truth. It would give her the closure her heart so deeply desired, while opening her eyes to all that was possible for her as the full descendant of the Seven Sisters.

Her aunt had told her that she was the key. Was she the mystery that would open the Legacy Lock once and for all?

CHAPTER TWENTY-NINE

THE MAP

Maple Moon was bustling, and Hannah didn't have a moment alone. When her shift was over, she headed straight back to the manor and sought out her aunt, who was in the library organizing stacks of books.

"Aunt Jewelia?"

"Yes, love?" Jewelia answered.

"You know that night when Jezebelle was ill and we went outside and spread ashes in the wind—to the moon? You led me down to the sea, to a place on the shore I hadn't been before, down the brook and across from the ash tree. I've wondered since then...why there?"

Jewelia's eyes perked up with deep knowing and reassurance. "You are right. It wasn't a coincidence or happenstance that we went to that location. There are places on this property, on the island, that are supercharged. Places of energetic overlap that some call ley lines. Remember when I showed you the map and how to find them?" Jewelia said, grabbing the large volume from a nearby bookshelf. "Divination being one, dowsing being another," she said, passing the ancient book to Hannah. "This map identifies all ley lines on the island. The spirals mark the precise points of their intersections."

"Oh yes, excellent, that eliminates all the guessing!" Hannah said excitedly, recognizing the synchronicity of spirals. "The labyrinths, I remember," Hannah confirmed, recalling when she had found one of them in the forest. Then the image of the map in her dream resurfaced, the one she was trying to decipher.

"My only caution is...make sure you are at the right spot, as these are very powerful locations, not to be accessed with impunity." Jewelia's gaze now took on a look of warning.

"I see." Hannah's excitement waned slightly as she held the map, her eyes scanning corner to corner.

"We were at this one, right?" she asked, pointing to a spot where the lines crossed one another on the shore.

Jewelia nodded. "Yes, but remember, they are all connected. Like power lines running down a street, one feeds into the others. In fact, the manor was purposely built at the convergence of these powerful ley lines."

"But how did they do that?"

"Have you ever heard of the theory of archeoastronomy? Stonehenge is a great example of this. They built certain structures to coincide with astronomical events. Similarly, there is astrocartography, which is essentially merging astrology with the science of maps to identify places to visit or move that resonate, based on celestial guidance."

"So, our ancestors used astrocartography to locate Maple Hollow, and then mapped the stars to gauge where to build the manor?"

"Yes. It has been said that these locations have the ability to defy the constraints of 3D reality: gravity, time, and space. There are those who believe that time warps exist at these intersections. For this reason, it is common for disappearances to occur at these locations, as well as other mysterious phenomena."

"If they are basically combining geology with astronomy, are the ley lines connected to the stars?"

"Of course they are. It is one large circular grid that is all connected."

"I've always felt a connection to the stars," Hannah told her. "In fact, certain ones in particular. I find myself looking for them. It's as if they signal a remembrance in my cells."

"And it is also why you were drawn here. When we view the ley lines on the map, we see that Skye Manor is built upon a powerful intersection point."

"It wasn't just my recurring pumpkin patch dream," Hannah said. "I mean, I came here to help find you, but there was much more going on energetically than that."

"Yes, there was, my love," Jewelia confirmed. "In addition to the ley lines, there are additional lines of power that exist within each one of us, just beneath our auric field. Those are called hara lines. These energy lines are what connect the stars and the Earth, with us in between, everyone has one. When we are aligned with our true calling and life's purpose, our hara line is aligned as well. When this happens, our life is filled with synchronicities and we can follow the discoveries much more easily."

"Can Grandpa's compass clock locate the ley lines?"

"I bet it can. As both a clock and a compass, it can probably detect the intersections."

Hannah had never before heard of hara lines. But it all made sense, especially with the concept of interconnectedness and quantum entanglement. She was following the discoveries. There had been synchronicity after synchronicity. She began to feel in her soul that her connection with the stars was aligned, and that her true calling and purpose were soon to be revealed.

She parted ways with Jewelia and stepped out into the hallway. To unlock the Legacy Lock, she would need to gather up items that represented each of the riddles. Each one of the riddles was a clue to a metaphorical key representing one of the Sisters of Skye, each sister an ambassador for that aspect of energy. And each one could help her solve the mystery of that seventh key.

What was the first key? The first riddle had foretold her discovery of the tunnels:

I Cannot Help but Run
Through the Channels I Churn
A Ladder I Descend
Darkness at Every Turn

Hannah ran to the pumpkin patch.

She had discovered her connection to the vines when she'd first arrived in Maple Hollow, and she instinctively knew this would be the first key. Standing in the center of the patch, she performed the ritual of carefully selecting one of the pumpkins to detach its vine. It sparkled in her hand, which tingled as she placed the vine in her black velvet pouch. Then she sat down in the soil and thanked the patch.

The sun was beginning to sink toward the Western horizon, and the most important of nights would be upon them soon. She closed her eyes, waiting for the next clue. The night before the ball, she had received the second riddle:

A Closed Hand Cannot Receive

A Distrusting Heart Cannot Relieve

Spun Within the Salty Tide

The Soul's Song Cannot Be Denied

But how could you gather a song? Or capture a note in the physical realm? She had used frequencies before to open a lock by playing a specific combination of notes Wixby had told her. That was *The Soul's Song.*

She jumped up and ran inside to the parlor and the grand piano. She would gather a piano string, but which one? She remembered when Seren had told her to hold a high vibration. The bass copper strings vibrated at a lower frequency, while the steel treble wire vibrated higher. And the treble clef was part of the Skye family crest. Recalling the technique she had learned in music school, Hannah used the tuning key to gradually loosen the tension on all of the pins, turning them until she could finally release one of the wires, and place it in her pouch.

As she sat on the piano bench, she stared into the fireplace and waited for the next direction.

Remove the Mask

Embrace the Power

Face the Flames

At the Final Hour

These were the words of the riddle she received after the ball. All this time, she had thought it was referring to the fire at Madame Morgans, or the fire that destroyed Norma Nyx, The Dream Haunter, but she had begun to doubt that. As she pondered what to do next, she heard the hoot of an owl outside. She stood up and looked out the window at the majestic maple trees that crowded the grounds. Suddenly, her phone beeped and interrupted her concentration. It was a notification from her celestial app.

"Flares...are...flames," she said out loud. The third riddle wasn't about facing the flames of Norma's destruction. It was about the solar flames that cause the aurora—celestial flames. The sun was one big ball of fire that gave life to everything on the planet. Without it, there would be no plants, no trees. What better way to represent it than through trees.

She ran outside and up to the first large tree she encountered. She snatched a glowing red leaf off a low branch, thanking it in her mind for its donation. She placed the leaf in her pouch and walked back into the house.

As she walked, she contemplated the fourth riddle, which had come through her and Ashlin at the library:

Cold as the Winter Branch
Warm as the Summer Sun
Count the Bridge of Autumn
To be an Enlightened One

She'd thought at first it was about the seasons, but then she'd considered the mention of a bridge and realized that the references to cold versus warm, and being an *Enlightened One*, was about opening her heart. She had experienced this not only when the lightning delivered a jolt of electricity to her body, but also when she had held Nutmeg, her connection to cats.

"That's it, of course. Whiskers!" It was like a lightbulb had popped above her head, illuminating her mind. She reached in her pocket and, to her surprise, there was a tiny white whisker.

There needs to be a bridge, she told herself, but between what? Summer and winter? Life and death? Light and dark?

After a moment, she realized that since Samhain is a cross-quarter celebration of the year, perhaps she needed to represent both the light and dark parts of consciousness by gathering both a light and dark whisker. Nutmeg's whisker was white, but she knew just where to get a black whisker—Midnight.

Hannah ran back inside, to her bedroom, and straight for the blanket Midnight always slept on. And right there, in the folds of the quilt, was a whisker. She gently grasped it and put it in her pouch. When she did, she saw the small crystals she had found in the tunnel on her nightstand. And the next riddle replayed in her mind.

I Cannot Be Seen
I Can Only Be Heard
Shift Dark to Light
Embody the Spoken Word

Ironically, this was the only riddle that she *did* see, as it had appeared on the mirror. The Clear Quartz is translucent; it's spectral crystalline structure almost ethereal. If the stones can protect against dark energy, then they can shift dark to light. And if the riddles *do* correlate to the chakras, this one would be associated with the throat. One's voice is itself, a frequency, embodied and heard. And what could be more indicative of becoming an enlightened one, than activating one's voice, embodying one's truth, and empowering true self-expression? She felt the crystal must be the key to the riddle, and snagged it off the cabinet, placing it securely in her pouch.

Then Hannah thought about the sixth riddle. She had thought it was about Varlina and Delvina because of the line mentioning twins:

Guides at Night
We Began as Twins
Where Duality Ends
A Third Begins

She thought back to when she had meditated upon the mum flower, when the energy reader had explained the chakras to her, and when Seren had told her the benefits of the Firestone—namely, that it can *awaken the third eye*. She also thought about the power outage they'd experienced at the manor, and her time in the tunnels—both times she had to find her way in the dark. She had pondered all the dualities of this existence she could consider...all but one. A shiver traveled through her body as a new thought emerged.

The sixth riddle was not about twins at all, it was about eyes, her eyes. They were the twins, her guides at night, allowing her to see through the darkness. Beyond her eyes, beyond their duality, was her inner vision, her dream vision, and that emanated from her intuition—her third eye. When her third eye was activated, it relieved the duties of her two physical eyes. That is where duality ends!

But how could she gather her third eye to put it with the other keys? She knew Delvina's painting must be part of the puzzle. Delvina had been painting with her eyes closed. She had been channeling through her third eye. Hannah realized she could use Delvina's brush to embody it.

Hannah left the manor, heading straight to the lounge.

"Merry Samhain!" Delvina said smiling as she passed the wrapped canvas to Hannah upon her arrival.

"Same to you! I can't wait to hang this up at the dinner tonight. Thanks again and see you there!" Hannah said obligingly, feeling special that the twins had saved it just for her.

"Would you mind if I kept one of your brushes...for good luck?"

"You're more than welcome to it," Delvina obliged, passing one to Hannah.

As Hannah left, the six keys in her pouch, her mind raced about what she was going to do with them. How would she uncover the seventh key and solve the Legacy Lock before midnight?

Stepping outside, she took out her phone and dialed Ashlin. She was going to see her tonight at the Silent Supper, but she couldn't wait to share what she had discovered.

"I've solved all the riddles but one," she said excitedly.

"How did you find the keys?" Ashlin hung on her words.

"I'll explain when I see you tonight, oh and the spirals in the prophecy, they're a paradox—the *coincidentia oppositorum!*"

"The coincidence of opposites? How?" Ashlin responded.

"I discovered it in the *Grimoire de Hollow.* As dissonant and uncompromising in opposition certain things may seem, they are in fact not as diametrically opposed as we believe them to be."

"Then what's the paradox?" Ashlin asked.

"It's like Jewelia said at the ball. Death is not opposite of life," Hannah said slowly, with a full realization. "When we can attain an enlightened consciousness, the paradox is solved."

"Solved how? How can they not be opposite?"

"Think about the whole concept of death as we know it. We think death and life are on opposite ends of the spectrum, but in fact the spectrum is a circle. What if the circle of life is...a spiral," she said as she traced a shape in the air with her finger. "The two ends are much closer together than we think."

"They aren't linear," she said, catching on.

"Right, in fact, they touch. All life is interconnected, like Celtic knotwork, intertwined and infinite."

CHAPTER THIRTY

THE SILENT SUPPER

It was finally the evening of Samhain, and all the children on the island were running from house to house, street to street, trick-or-treating. Everyone saved Skye Manor for last, looking forward to it all night long.

The sun began to set across the island, spattering pink, orange, and red across the clouds. The crickets started to chirp and the owls to hoot. Hannah, Jewelia, Wendy, and Old Man Adams took turns answering the door and dolling out candy and treats. Like the children, each of them was decked out in an elaborate costume for the occasion.

As the trick-or-treaters started to subside, the slam of the doorknocker became less and less frequent. An eerie silence began to build within the manor. It was nearly time for the Silent Supper, where they would open a portal for spirits to cross the veil between the worlds. Varlina and Delvina had passed out formal parchment invitations, embossed with the Skye Manor wax seal, to everyone who had attended the art exhibit. The invitations explicitly stated the expectations: the supper would commence at 11 p.m. All guests were required to conceal their identity by wearing a cloak and mask. No speaking, nor conversation, was allowed between any of the guests until the supper was completed. As the intent was to dine with the dead, everyone was instructed to write, on the back of their invitation, a message to someone who had passed on. They were then to bring their invitation with them to the supper and present it at the door for admission, then place it inside the large hollowed-out pumpkin.

A gentle breeze blew the dried leaves from their branches, swirling them downward in the moonlight as the guests arrived. One by one, the cars pulled up the driveway. Old Man Adams, now dressed in freshly ironed black butler attire, attended to the arrivals, opening the door for each and welcoming them in.

As each guest entered, a thick sense of mystery filled the foyer. They silently milled about into the parlor, observing the ancient interior and its elaborate decorations. Large lanterns lined the pathways between the rooms, casting dark shadows.

Some wandered about the great hall, observing the statues and the ornate organ carved out of maple wood adorned with gothic flowers and skulls, its dragon-clawed feet holding it up against the towering wall behind it, upon which keys of every size were hung. And over the grand fireplace now hung Delvina's special painting, the masterpiece of both spirit and feline inspiration.

When the grandfather clock reached the top of the hour, Jewelia struck a small gong to gain attention and motioned for everyone to follow her into the great hall to take their seats. One by one, the guests made their way to the expansive table filled with Wendy's opulent delicacies. A large fire crackled in the fireplace, emitting a musky smoke into the chimney. The smell of melted wax, incense, and spices wafted in the air.

Each person took their seat, leaving the head of the table empty as an invitation for those who have passed on. Each place setting featured black dishes and black linens, and was set in reverse: each sparkling silver spoon, fork, and knife on the opposite side, each glass similarly placed in opposition. Large rectangular centerpieces displayed white and orange pumpkins, acorns, gourds with bumpy skin, ripe winter squash, crisp apples, sliced persimmons, and pomegranates bearing their seeds, all intermingled with flaming orange chrysanthemums. Tall, black-branched arrangements stretched up from them, flanked by dried twigs and moss.

Once everyone had taken their seat, Jewelia stood at the far end of the table and held up a large, ancient-looking hourglass. She turned it upside down and sat it in front of the empty chair. This marked the time for the dinner hour.

Since no words could be spoken, she remained silent. Telepathy took hold, as some of the guests seemed to hold conversations with each other without exchanging auditory sounds.

To bring the dead back to the living, and remove the linear order of time, all courses of the meal were served in reverse, starting with a steamy apple-spice tart, its decadent, flaky crust moist from its oozing, sweet fruit. The main course was a steamy wild mushroom risotto topped with roasted garlic and crispy sage.

Once everyone ate their fill of the risotto, the appetizer was served, a mixed greens salad of bitter arugula, braised pear, and burnt-honey beets topped with candied walnuts. As the sand in the hourglass was nearly at its end, each guest was served a large piece of generously spiced pumpkin bread.

Wendy rose from her chair and helped Old Man Adams clear away the plates. Hannah walked out to the foyer to retrieve the pumpkin by the door that was filled with the invitations.

When she returned to the great hall, she walked slowly around the perimeter of the table, grasping the pumpkin close to her chest. Then she walked to the fireplace, turned the opening of the pumpkin toward the fire, and tipped it out so the messages to the spirits, scrawled on the parchments, met the reaching flames.

Everyone watched in solemn silence as their message was enveloped by the fire. The sparks raced up the chimney and the smoke rose like ghostly fingers up toward Delvina's painting. Then they all sat watching, waiting, their eyes closely observing each other. Some had looks of suspicion, some of relief, some of satisfaction.

Hannah watched the painting and observed the spiral at the center beginning to turn. The messages had activated the painting's portal. She had a flash of realization. On her invitation, she had asked for the solution to the last riddle, and in her mind now, she saw the compass clock.

It would guide her to the crossroads. The sacred intersection she sought. She submerged her hand into her pouch to grasp it, where she had put it with the keys she had collected.

There wasn't much time left before the strike of midnight, the *Shadow Hour.* But before Jewelia could make her announcement that the supper was concluded, there was a sudden and alarming burst of movement. An ominous-looking masked man stood up and broke the silence.

CHAPTER THIRTY-ONE

THE DIMENSIONS

"My wish is granted. The transference of power. From all of you, to me, at this shadow hour!" he pronounced, sneering. He grabbed the hourglass and ripped off his mask, revealing his thick eyebrows and menacing angular face.

As soon as she saw his piercing eyes, Hannah's suspicions were confirmed. It was the watcher from the Masquerade Ball and from the streets outside Maple Moon. He had been at the exhibit, and she felt surer than ever that he had been down in the tunnels with her.

Everyone gasped in shock and bewilderment. Not only because he was the first to speak all night, but also because they realized he had something terrible planned. He definitely wasn't just a tourist or an art collector. He wasn't a curious reveler partaking in their annual celebration.

"Zekerias?" Jewelia said, her eyes wide.

"Jewelia?" Hannah gasped. Was this the man standing next to her father in the photo? The one her aunt was so wanting to escape?

"You have no power here," Jewelia declared swiftly. Before Hannah could say anything, Zekerias ran out of the great hall and up the grand staircase with the hourglass.

"Stop him!" Jewelia yelled, hoping someone could grab or trip him on the way. Old Man Adams spun around and lunged, but it was too late. The unmasked man was bounding up the stairs at top speed.

Hannah immediately ran after him, Midnight in tow. "To the turret!" she yelled back down the stairs behind her.

Jewelia, Morgan, Ashlin, Seren, Varlina, Delvina, and Wendy all went storming up the stairs in pursuit, while the rest of the guests swarmed about in confusion, chattering and speculating on what had taken place.

But no one could catch him. Zekerias ran straight up into the turret room, clutching the hourglass. Hannah was close behind him, and as soon as he threw open the door, he ran to the middle of the room and heaved the heavy hourglass onto the floor, smashing it into tiny pieces and scattering the sand. When he did, the sand spread out into a circle surrounding him and the entire floor began to shake like there was an earthquake. The circular floor broke off from the surrounding walls and began slowly rotating clockwise.

Hannah attempted to run into the room, but the rotating floor created a force field that blew her and Midnight back through the doorway. The others crammed behind her as they reached the top of the stairs, mirroring the clamoring crowd in her dream.

"Tonight is a monumental intersection of dimensions!" Zekerias declared coldly. "I have been patiently waiting for this time to come. Now that the keys have been gathered, the Wheel of Skye can spin freely." He held his arms up in the air in satisfaction. "The wheel is beyond the limitations of time, space, and distance, catalyzing multi-dimensional power. Now I will defeat time. I will become immortal. No one can destroy me, and I will wield the forces of all keys forever."

All of the moisture evaporated from Hannah's mouth, as she realized her friends and family weren't the only ones who knew about the prophecy. Her breathing became shallow when she finally got a closer look at the tattoo on his arm. It was a circle with a triangle and a snake inside. The very same symbol she had seen on the Dream Haunters. Was he one of them? Had he simply been waiting for her to gather the keys? Was someone going to die in this room, as the prophecy foretold?

"You're a Dream Haunter!" Hannah declared, but Zekerias sneered.

"You still don't get it, do you?" he quipped. "I am the rightful heir of this legacy."

"I always suspected you were wicked, Zekerias!" Jewelia yelled, angry that she had denied her intuition all those years.

"You'll never get away with this," Morgan told him, shaking her fist.

Suddenly everyone else was chiming in, agreeing and threatening the intruder, pushing for entrance to the room.

Hannah knew he was part of an evil secret society, Dream Haunter or not. But she also was suddenly beginning to realize, by claiming birthright, he was revealing his relation to the Seven Sisters somehow. Was he part of one of the families?

"What do you mean, rightful heir…of who?" Hannah demanded an answer.

Then suddenly, Hannah watched in horror as glass columns descended from the ceiling in the hallway to encase each person where they stood. As they came down, everyone seemed to fall into a trance, not resisting, just succumbing to the entrapment. Old Man Adams stood perfectly still, a dumbfounded look on his face. Jewelia's eyes were closed, as if she was listening to a beautiful song. Wendy was moving her mouth as if savoring a delectable treat. Ashlin, Seren, and Morgan appeared to be concentrating intently, but on what Hannah could not tell.

"My mother was one of the Seven Sisters, I am Zekerias Danua, the only living heir."

Hannah's eyes became wide as she looked at Ashlin, wondering if she could hear.

"She insisted I could not wield the power, so I made it my life mission to prove her wrong. I coveted her powers; she was connected to the elements of the earth and vibrational frequencies. When she passed, I learned everything I could about the other families, including yours, planning my takeover for many years." Then he positioned himself in a prideful stance and began to ominously chant.

"Beckoning Darkness, Summoning Fright
Time Stops on This Special Night
Keep You Here in This Very Room
Ignorance Sealing Your Ultimate Doom."

"What's happening to them?" Hannah yelled at him.

"These are time loops, traps to keep them uninquisitive. It's better for everyone involved. They'll never know what they're missing."

"No, you can't trap them!" Hannah said in desperation and fear. In the back of her mind, she was waiting for a column to descend over her.

"I'm afraid it's already done. They can't protect you anymore. Neither can the Seven Sisters," he said, sneering at her threateningly. "We bequeathed that those women and their descendants would all suffer a great loss, which you have. We also commanded that your body would revolt against you, which I see is working splendidly." He grinned at Hannah. "I have been trying to get to this room for years. At first, I thought my girlfriend Jaime would be my ticket in, but she wouldn't go along with my plan. Jezebelle was easy to convince, blinded by pride, but she didn't succeed. I had to take matters into my own hands," he scoffed.

"It was me in the dark tunnels. I tried to trap you there. While you were distracted, gathering rocks, I snuck back up the ladder and locked the trap door from the inside. At the Masquerade Ball, I tried to poison you, first with tainted appetizers snuck onto the table, and then with a spiked drink, but each time you were distracted away. I knew I had to try something different, because fate was protecting you."

"It was you, at the gallery trying to buy Delvina's painting...why?" Hannah asked.

"Because I realized that Delvina's painting is a portal, her brushes are a conduit between the worlds. Now that you have done all the work for me, gathering each piece together, the culmination is at hand. There will be no future sisters. Your power stops here!"

"Culmination!" Hannah exclaimed as Midnight jumped into her arms. She realized Zekerias knew about the Midnight Culmination, the zenith of the Pleiades. "*Your* ancestors are the reason *my* ancestors left their homeland and sought refuge here. Your ancestors enacted the curse!" she said fiercely.

"Yes, the curse is two-fold, but you already figured that out. In the women, as their power grows, so does a sickness that works against it, weakening and confusing them so they are distracted away from it. It worked on your aunt, your friend Morgan, and even my own mother."

"Jewelia? Morgan? So, you're the reason Jewelia couldn't fight off the Dream Haunters? And why Morgan was trapped by the Illusionix?"

"Now you're getting it," he growled. Midnight began pawing at Hannah's face, trying to get her attention.

"And the men? What's the curse on them?" Hannah asked, realizing perhaps the cats weren't part of the curse.

"Each generation is gradually reduced by eliminating them, of course. My father and yours, your grandfather, and their fathers before them. Each generation, until they ultimately die out." He paced slowly around the rotating wheel, observing the phenomenon. "That's why I befriended, and ultimately destroyed, your father."

"The accident...you caused it? You killed my parents?"

"I had to make sure your parents couldn't create any more offspring, the combination was just too powerful."

Hannah's body stiffened, her mouth falling open in shock. Midnight leapt from her arms and ran to the glass columns. "What combination?" she said in a shaky voice, knowing he was probably talking about her. But he didn't answer.

"You kept getting in the way, so I had to come destroy you myself. This room is the intersection of the most powerful ley lines known on Earth, and it represents the cosmic wheel of time, which can only be awakened by activating keys from all dimensions. I know you have them, so insert the keys," he demanded, pointing at six keyholes dispersed around the wheel.

"You lured us up here so you could manifest the power of the turret to do your bidding," Hannah said, her muscles tightening.

"It's quite simple. I've been trying to harness this power for years. I tried to destroy the ancient book of wisdom at Maple Moon. In fact, that's why I caused the fire. If I can rule the Wheel of Skye, I can control time and space. Everyone will forget their power, and I can capture it all for myself. I can be the most powerful being, limitless beyond measure."

Hannah was slowly putting it together. She began to understand the revelations of the riddles more deeply. Each riddle represented a dimension of existence that, all together, created what we know as reality. Without each of these dimensions, reality would cease to exist. She had unraveled the clues and gathered the items representing each dimension. And the turret was the intersection of all the ley lines.

"And what if I stop you?" she challenged him. She knew her hara line, and her greater purpose, were in alignment with the universe, and that Zekerias was not. She understood the heart was the bridge between worlds, not the ego. She noticed that Midnight was now forcefully scratching at the ground in front of the columns, attempting to free Jewelia and the others.

"You can try," Zekerias chuckled. "Everyone you know and care about will be trapped in their own time loop forever."

Hannah looked down the hallway at Jewelia, Morgan, Ashlin, Seren, Varlina, Delvina, and Wendy. Each one of them frozen. What choice did she have? But how could she fight Zekerias alone? He had killed her parents, and now he might succeed in killing her, too. She had the keys, but she didn't want to unlock the Wheel of Skye at Zekerias' orders. She still couldn't believe that this sacred wheel, named after her family, had laid dormant inside the pinnacle of her ancestral manor this whole time.

The thought crossed her mind, that maybe if she did insert them, that the seventh key would reveal itself. Hannah unhooked the small velvet pouch she had looped around her wrist and began to insert each item into the keyholes as they slowly spun past, muttering in disgust. First the small piece of the pumpkin vine. When she inserted it, the keyhole began to glow with a bright white light. Hannah then reached for the piano string, threading it into the next keyhole. Again, bright light emanated forth. Next was the maple leaf. She folded it in half, inserting it into the third keyhole.

"It's working!" Zekerias proclaimed, pleased with himself.

As she stood in front of the turning wheel, almost half of it strongly glowing, Hannah thought about her parents. How could this person who now stood in front of her, who had been responsible for changing the entire course of her life, leaving her parentless, get away with this? Was she going to let this happen?

She pulled out the remaining items. The whiskers: one white, Nutmeg's, and one black, Midnight's. Together they represented the light and the dark she had battled within herself. She had discovered that her connection with cats was the bridge to her heart. Midnight meowed when his discarded whisker touched the lock.

"It's okay, Midnight," Hannah tried to reassure him.

And last, the Clear Quartz crystal she had found in the tunnel and the paintbrush from the lounge.

"Good, now back away!" Zekerias yelled. The wheel began to spin faster.

"Beyond all limits of space and time, I hereby declare these powers as mine!" he proclaimed as all six keyholes glowed brightly. But then he seemed to falter. "Something's wrong," he said angrily.

Hannah realized in a flash that even though Zekerias was a descendant of the seventh family, he didn't have the high vibration required to solve the mystery. He didn't know what the seventh key was.

She had gathered six keys and placed them in the holes of the Legacy Lock on the Wheel of Skye: the pumpkin vine, the piano string, the maple leaf, the cat whiskers, the Clear Quartz crystal, and the paintbrush. Each one of the riddles had revealed a dimension of existence, which had led her to discover a key. The elemental dimension of the soil, the frequency dimension of the soul's song, the solar dimension of the island's trees, the mineral dimension of magickal stones, the animal dimension that was the bridge to her heart, and the artistic dimension channeled through the third eye of consciousness. But the seventh dimension...she wasn't even sure how to understand it. The only things left in her pouch were the small bottle of elixir from Seren and the compass clock.

Could she open the Legacy Lock before Zekerias did? What stood between herself and everything she didn't know?

Hannah felt a wave of knowing sweep over her. She took Seren's elixir from her pocket and stood silently with it in her hand. She unscrewed the glistening top of the shimmering vial and brought it to her mouth. The liquid was shiny and thick. It slowly began to swirl and adhere to gravity, sliding its way toward her lips.

Before she knew it, the elixir met the warmth of her mouth and was swirling around her tongue. It tasted sweet and nourishing. Hannah quickly swallowed, allowing it to fill her throat, rapidly spreading a wave of warmth toward her heart and lungs. As the liquid passed into her body, she felt her aura begin to glow. She could feel the elixir making its way down to her stomach, into the pit of her core. It began to warm her entire body with a tingly expansiveness she'd never felt before.

The wheel began to spin faster and faster. Zekerias tried to steady himself, but was becoming confused and disoriented.

Then she remembered what Wixby had told her about his experience with time travel. And what Morgan had told her when she had first come to the island, about cats living in a netherworld between worlds. They could "blink," traveling beyond space and time.

Aunt Jewelia had once told her the turret room was a portal that could transport people to places as well as transport things to people. *Whatever the universe needs you to see can appear in that room*, she had said. Hannah thought back to the last time she'd been in the turret room, with Ashlin. She'd declared it a protected space: *No darkness shall dwell here nor attach itself,* she had proclaimed. Zekerias could not control the wheel.

Hannah called upon the spirits of the cats she had known in the physical realm: her first cat, Mystera, and all the cats of Maple Hollow: Midnight, Milu, Merlin, Lirean, Nutmeg, and Zooti, the elder forest cat. She also called upon all of her guides to help her: Wixby, Abernathy, Leaf, and all the owls who had appeared in her dreams. Midnight stopped his scratching and ran to Hannah as a multitude of glowing eyes appeared around her, illuminating the darkness. She repeated the final riddle in her mind, summoning the quantum dimension:

I Grow in the Garden
I Fill Up a Room
Faster Than Music
You Will Discover it Soon

It seemed so obvious, now that she had consumed the elixir. Hannah asked herself why she hadn't thought of this before. The maple leaf had been the key of the solar dimension, but she hadn't thought of herbs—one herb that grows in a garden is thyme. She pondered, *I Fill Up a Room.* What could fill up a room, besides the large wheel before her? Space! Time and space.

And what was faster than music? The speed of sound, of course. The seventh key was the elixir, a gateway to the quantum realm. It was the quantum key, which would allow her to transcend both time and space, stepping through the circular portal of time itself, which was not linear at all.

Hannah reached inside her bag for the compass clock and began envisioning the seven spirals from the mirror.

"Access the Timeline in Between," she pronounced as the wheel began to spin faster and faster. "Unlock the Crossroads under the Darkest Skies." Her voice dropped to a whisper in amazement. Midnight was standing up on his back legs, reaching into the air, conjuring a spinning cyclone of sparkling air with his paws. The compass clock hands oscillating out of control.

The wheel began to spin even faster, catching Zekerias in a violent spiral. His face began to stretch, the skin struggling to envelope his deformation. His hands reached out to stop Hannah from speaking, but they too began to stretch out like rubber bands, snapping back upon himself. He became thin and long, his physical form squished and flattened until there was nothing of Zekerias left.

The turret room was the convergence of all of the key ley lines. It was a vortex, a portal beyond time and space. And it had destroyed Zekerias, once and for all.

"Unlock the legacy of our power!" Hannah intoned. Her voice began to rise, growing louder and louder, filling her lungs, channeling her spirit into the keyholes. The wheel began to slow down and separate from the floorboards, rising up to stand before her, then the keyholes receded and a doorway appeared, with a large ornate knob.

Hannah placed her hand on the knob and gently twisted it open. Walking through the doorway, she found herself standing in the foyer of the manor. She stepped out of sight, hiding behind a draped curtain at the entrance of the parlor.

For the first time in her entire existence on this planet, she saw herself. She was walking out to the foyer to retrieve the pumpkin that everyone had deposited their invitations in. Hannah stood as still as a statue.

She almost didn't recognize herself, since her appearance was so very different than what she had always seen in the mirror. Seeing herself from a 3D perspective was entrancing. She couldn't look away, and yet she knew her physical form was a distraction from her mission, and that if she succumbed to focusing on it, she might miss this crucial time-gap opportunity.

She looked at the grandfather clock. It was rotating at a faster rate. Time was moving faster than usual. As she observed time race past her, she realized that it appeared everyone was eating the supper courses in the usual order, not in reverse, and the sand in the hourglass was not moving down from the top glass ball to the bottom one, but actually from the bottom to the top, defying gravity. She was moving backward in time. She could get the hourglass, before Zekerias did. While everyone was distracted by the delectable dishes, she averted her eyes and smoothly passed through the room, removed the hourglass from the head of the table, and then sprinted up the multiple flights of stairs to the turret.

Once back in the room, she carefully placed the hourglass in the center of the circular floor. Then she closed her eyes and visualized the Wheel of Skye. It was time to give her voice to the prophecy.

"I Separate but Also Allow," she said, realizing that doors separate things but also allow access. She had traveled back in time a few minutes by crossing the threshold of the quantum doorway.

"I Stand in Silence Until You Know How." Hannah understood now this referred to her ability to activate all of the energy centers within herself, to raise her consciousness and vibration high enough to travel beyond time.

"With Just a Twist, Reveal the Unseen," she continued.

Remembering that Wixby had told her to look to the sky, Hannah looked up and found that the roof of the turret room was now transparent glass, and she could see the whole expansive night sky through it. As she scanned the skies, her eyes went to the seven stars of the Pleiades, which began to glow and spin and descend from the top of the turret down into the Wheel of Skye. Glowing sets of cat eyes appeared, surrounding the circle. Light began to emanate from beneath her, rising up in her body to the crown of her head.

Hannah closed her eyes and began to look through her third eye. A cloud of mist and shimmery fog appeared, and out of it, a figure approached, arms extended. It was her mother.

"Mom?" Hannah said, unsure.

"Yes, Hannah, it's me," her mom said reassuringly, smiling as they embraced. Then she stepped back and gazed at her daughter. "We're so sorry we weren't there for you. We wanted to protect you, but we didn't realize you had powers that were envied by evil forces. They tried to destroy us, to destroy you, and to keep you from carrying on the family legacy of power." She put an arm around Hannah's shoulders. "You have discovered the Skye lineage that is your father's, my dear. Since it is passed down through female children, you had to be born to continue it, but he unfortunately did not have the magick himself. That is why he dismissed your Aunt Jewelia. He didn't understand what he could not personally possess. But what you didn't know about was my lineage," she added, smiling.

"Are you a Healer of the Hollow, too?" Hannah asked. "But how could..." She trailed off as her mother held her forefinger to her lips.

"My lineage is of the stars. You, Hannah, are a starseed. The Pleiades is a star cluster in the fifth dimension. The closest star cluster to Earth, it is still nearly 444 light years away. Didn't you always feel different, ever since you were a child? Did you ever wonder why you were having such vivid dreams growing up?"

"I did," Hannah confirmed.

"Pleiadeans are stewards of spiritual awakening who incarnate on the Earth in the third dimension. Compassionate ambassadors for the transformation of the collective, we are messengers of enlightenment. We are extremely sensitive, telepathic, strongly intuitive, creative, and carry deep wisdom of the shadow realm. Pleiadeans are natural healers, strongly connected to animals and nature."

Hannah was resonating with amazement.

"Have you ever felt like you had a deeper purpose here? Did you ever feel out of place in the world, but when you gaze at the night sky, you find a fond sense of remembrance? When you incarnated into this world, you agreed to an amnesia of your origin, but the lesson here is the remembering."

Speechless, her heart was overflowing with exhilaration not only from seeing her mother, but from realizing that everything she knew to be innately true about herself was real, validated. She did feel different as a child. She'd had amazingly vivid dreams ever since she could remember. Her mother's words resonated so deeply within her soul that it was like a rock-solid foundation of resilience was forming underneath her. She never wanted to lose this feeling.

Her mother continued. "Our celestial ancestors brought seeds from the stars and placed them in the earth of this planet. They spread underground into rivers of ore, metallic streams of gold, silver, bronze, and iron coursing deep below the surface," she said, admiring the sparking glow of the stars.

"We are starseeds, children of those ancestors, descendants of the stars. We agreed to be birthed on this Earth as part of a cosmic contract to be fulfilled. To do our work, we accepted the sacrifice that our memories, as well as recollections of past existences, would be removed to reside beyond the veil."

"So, we all have ancestral amnesia?" Hannah asked.

"It is not completely wiped from existence, as all things happen in parallel, but it is enough out of reach that we can chose to ignore or dismiss it and carry on unaware, in a state of ignorant bliss. This is the ignorance Zekerias has trapped everyone in tonight. But if we choose to pull back the veil, to reconnect with the memories of our legacy, it is a choice to raise our spiritual intelligence. In doing so, we are not discovering, but remembering."

"I do remember now. I always knew this, but I had forgotten," Hannah confirmed.

"Your name is a palindrome, Hannah," her mother continued. "It is the same forward as it is backward. It is also a mirror onto itself. In the middle, is you. You were named such because you were chosen as a time traveler. You have the ability to move seamlessly forward and backward in time. This is because you have ascended to a level that is beyond space and time. You understand and have surpassed these 3D limitations. We have been waiting in the quantum to be reunited."

"We?" Hannah said, looking up.

"Hello, Hannah," said her father's voice, and then her eyes met with his.

"Dad?" she said in disbelief, her heart surging with excitement.

"Yes, Hannah, it's me." He reached out his arms for her as they embraced.

"Dad, I've missed you so much," Hannah told him, tears welling up in her eyes.

"I'm always here, even when you can't see me. Death is not the opposite of life. Souls don't die; we just live in the quantum realm beyond sight and sound. It is all within and of us. Nothing is above or below," he explained. "I'm sorry I kept you from discovering your power. All I ever wanted was to protect you. I thought if I hid the truth of your legacy, you would be able to live out your life safely, free from harm. They wanted to destroy all of us."

"They?" Hannah asked. "Who? The Dream Haunters or the Illusionix?"

Her father shook his head. "The real evil are the Keepers."

"Who?" Hannah asked again, confused.

"Some call them The Keepers of the Cage. Rulers of Phantasm, they enforce the confines of 3D reality. Things like space and time wouldn't hold sway without them. They want to keep humanity ignorant, complacent, naive. Many years ago, the Keepers cursed our family. They knew eventually our power would grow and combine with other power systems to become too powerful for them to destroy. When that happened, and the chosen one was born, humanity's consciousness would begin to shift, moving toward a greater awakening. This would destabilize their hold, putting everything they enforced at risk."

"So, the Dream Haunters are minions of The Keepers of the Cage?" Hannah surmised.

"Yes, amongst many others. The Keepers have legions of evil forces whose mission is solely to prevent the awakening of the masses. They had to make sure your mother and I didn't have any more offspring."

"You mean, they caused your car accident?"

"Yes. Because Halloween and Mercury retrograde overlapped that year, they were able to materialize and maliciously hijack our car. That is also why they sent the Dream Haunters and the Illusionix after you and the others."

"And Zekerias...is he a minion as well?" Hannah asked.

Her father nodded. "He is...now, but he wasn't always. Zekerias is an estranged descendant of the seventh family line. He was jealous and bitter that he did not inherit the powers, so he switched sides and joined the Keepers of the Cage. In exchange for this loyalty, they gave him the ability to encase others in a suspended state of time, unaware and powerless.

"But you changed all that, Hannah," her mother chimed in. "You are both a starseed and a Healer of the Hollow. You are a combination they never imagined would happen. The Seven Sisters each represented a spiral, an energetic signature. By embodying all of these dimensions, you activated all of their power within yourself. The Keepers now do not have power over you. You have upgraded your consciousness to the timeline of the New Earth, one where you can freely anchor into true alignment with your authentic, multi-dimensional self. Harness this opportunity to be a lighthouse for the world. A vibrant star in the vast night sky. We are always here for you, Hannah," her mother said as her father nodded.

"May the magickal realms illuminate your path," her father added, smiling.

Hannah felt the sweet truth of these words fill her spirit, from her feet to her heart and bursting out of the crown of her head into the world. It was true. She could move between the realms. She felt the foundation of her reality shifting beneath her as the deep realization recalibrated her mind, body, and spirit.

Slowly, the vision of her parents began to disappear into a shimmering cloud of starlight that led up into the sky and the glass columns vanished, freeing each person from their time loop captivity.

"Hannah, are you okay?" she heard from behind her.

She turned to see Ashlin, Morgan, Jewelia, Wendy, Seren, Delvina, Varlina, and Old Man Adams all now standing in the room with her.

"Yes...I..." She almost couldn't find words to speak.

She looked at Ashlin first, then Seren with a look of knowing. Morgan winked and Jewelia walked over to stand beside her.

"When you sent me your letter six years ago, and it said to *Save Our Legacy,* I thought it was about my father's heritage," Hannah said to her. "But I never thought there was more—that I was a starseed."

"You've discovered yet another mystery about your-self, dear," Morgan said. "When you aligned your chakras, you also activated your eighth, your Soul Star. This chakra moves your consciousness away from the egoic crown to the universal self, the universal heart of other dimensions."

"And I know who the Seven Sisters are, Zekerias' mother was one of them, her last name was Danua."

"Danua!" Old Man Adams blurted. That's my great grandmother's maiden name!"

Everyone spun around, shocked looks on their faces.

"You're a descendant of the Seven Sisters?!" Jewelia asked, wide-eyed and smiling.

"That explains so much," Ashlin exclaimed.

"My ancestors had powers, and I never knew! That's why I felt so close to your grandfather," he said to Hannah. "We had this affinity I could never explain. I had no idea, but now it all makes sense how I ended up here as a Protector of the Hollow."

"And we are so glad you did. This whole time, I knew we were family," Morgan remarked, and Jewelia nodded, both of them patting his arm in acceptance.

"That's amazing," Hannah beamed.

"So, we are all descendants of the seven sisters," Jewelia affirmed. "Their souls, and ours, agreed to reincarnate to raise the spiritual consciousness of the Earth. But you, my dear, are one of a kind," she said patting Hannah on the shoulder. "How did you figure all of this out?"

"The dimensions of the elements, frequencies, solar, animals, minerals, and art create a cosmic web," Hannah said, summarizing how she had gathered all of the riddles and keys. "When we activate our connection to these dimensions, we can surpass the constraints of space and time. No longer bound by what can be physically perceived, no longer limited by the spinning clock or the flipping calendar of hours, days, and years quickly passing. No longer constrained to the limited perception that life on this planet is all there is."

Ashlin chimed in. "The Sisters are not gone. They live on in all of us. To truly understand the earthly concept of death, we must cast away this entangled web—the cage of our consciousness."

"Those who discard or, even more so, fear the concept of consciousness outside our planet, who refuse to accept the overwhelming truth of vast galaxies, are minions of The Keepers of the Cage," Hannah pronounced.

"Their consorts are 3D space and time," Seren said thoughtfully.

"They cling to false illusory concepts," Delvina added, nodding.

Old Man Adams, his eyes twinkling with relief and happiness, began to sweep up the broken glass and sand. Each woman then moved toward the edge of the Wheel of Skye. One by one, they slowly walked around the perimeter of the circle. Unraveling the curse of ancestral demise. Hannah felt a knowing come from deep down inside herself, and she began to chant:

"Deirfiúracha inár n-anam

Bain na sean eagla

Ardaíonn ár spiorad anois

Athraíonn amlínte gan deireadh."

"Sisters in our soul

Remove the fear of old

Our spirits now ascend

Timelines shift with no end."

They navigated the wheel seven times. Then fog rose up from the center and snaked around each woman's ankles, enveloping their physical form.

EPILOGUE

Hannah pressed her palms to her eyes, then wiped and gently opened them. A lone owl hooted, acknowledging her awakening. She was outside the manor, in the pumpkin patch. The gentle sounds of crickets oscillated in her ears. Fireflies danced in a cloud above her head. And Midnight was circling around her, rubbing his face on her skin.

She stood up, finally realizing where she was. She ran to the hole in the ground that she had emerged from when she discovered the tunnels. But when she removed the grate Old Man Adams had placed there, she found only solid ground underneath. She and Midnight continued to check the area for openings, but they didn't find any. The underground tunnels were gone, and along with it, the fear they had brought.

She could hear the echoing sounds of celebrating voices coming from inside the great hall. Running to an outside window, she and Midnight cautiously peered in. But she did not see herself, nor Zekerias.

Everyone else was dancing and regaling, celebrating the arrival of Samhain, dressed in their Halloween best. Hannah remembered in an instant that she had shifted time. By unlocking the Legacy Lock, she had healed the ancestral wounds of the Seven Sisters and destroyed Zekerias, stretching him into oblivion inside the space/time continuum. By gathering all of the keys and walking the spiral seven times, the curse was broken and time was shifted. She had now ascended into a new embodied version of her universal self. One that was both a healer and a starseed.

She felt empowered in the realization that she was made of cosmic magick. She no longer felt the fog of confusion, weakness, and dis-ease that had plagued her. It was time to celebrate, knowing that her parents were always with her in spirit.

As she stood within the cluster of the maple trees outside the great Skye Manor, the bountiful pumpkins blossoming throughout the grounds and bats fluttering across the moon, her heart was full. The wind gently rustled the leaves in the trees. As her vibration rose higher and higher, the leaves started to loosen their grip, each one in its own time gently releasing its attachments, letting go. She watched the gleaming leaves drift on the night breeze, each one riding a stream of air, becoming bright orange monarchs. The glowing butterflies continued to burst from the trees, transforming from the falling leaves. It filled Hannah's heart with the most gentle, comforting feeling. Tears of joy came to her eyes as she watched their path up into the sky toward the moon, where they became twinkling stars in the night sky.

Then she turned and made her way through the crisp air toward the manor. Toward her family, friends, felines, and future.

ACKNOWLEDGMENTS

I would like to send a heartfelt thanks to my community of supportive and enlightened women who have shared their very personal awakening stories on my podcast, inspiring me to never give up in connecting to my universal wisdom; my audiobook narrator, Pearl Hewitt who brought this trilogy to life just as I imagined; my patient cover designer, Dragana Nikolic; my exemplary editors, Sandy Sullivan and Tina Dubois; my amazing Witches of Maple Hollow street team for your continual encouragement and promotion; and my felines, family, friends, and fellow writers who accompanied me on my author journey, it has made all the difference.

A NOTE TO THE READER

Dear Reader,

I hope you've enjoyed the third and final installment of the trilogy. If you'd like to be part of the Witches of Maple Hollow Community, I invite you to sign up for my newsletter, which will continue to evolve as an inspired space of magickal personal development and mystical guidance. I also hope you'll consider dropping a quick review of the trilogy at the retailer of your choice, as well as on Goodreads.

I love to connect with other women who are intrigued by metaphysics and who wish to delve into their dreams while raising their spiritual intelligence. Please reach out and share your experience—I'd love to hear it. Visit me at MeganMary.com and follow me @meganmaryauthor. Thank you again for your support.

Megan Mary

About the Author

Metaphysical author and dream analyst, Megan Mary, intertwines her passion for personal transformation, magick, and cats with the ethereal realm of dreams.

In addition to a career spanning over twenty-five years creating, managing and marketing websites, she holds a BA and an MA in English Literature, certification in British Studies, is pursuing her PhD in Metaphysical Sciences, and is a member of the International Association for the Study of Dreams.

After being diagnosed with three chronic illnesses, she experienced a spiritual awakening. She now empowers women all over the world to live more authentic, aligned, and abundant lives through dream empowerment and mystical guidance. Her podcast, Women's Dream Enlightenment, has been voted as one of the Top 20 Spiritual Awakening Podcasts You Must Follow. When she's not dreaming or weaving digital webs, she enjoys spending time with her husband and two magickal cats.

Follow @MeganMaryAuthor on Instagram, Threads, YouTube, Pinterest, X & TikTok